Kiss Goodbye

Jennifer Chapman

Fisher King Publishing

Fisher King Publishing
The Studio
Arthington Lane
Pool in Wharfedale
LS21 1JZ
England

www.fisherkingpublishing.co.uk

Also by Jennifer Chapman

Fiction

The Long Weekend
Mysterious Ways
Not Playing the Game
Regretting It
Victor Ludorum
Jeremy's Baby
I Know Who You Are

Non-fiction

The Last Bastion
Barnardo's Today
Made in Heaven

For Mrs Bennett

Chapter One

It was early, still dark. A man in a long black coat was standing by the bed, gently touching me.

I stirred, opened my eyes.

'I've made a mistake,' he was saying. 'With the ferry. I've made a mistake with the booking. The return is for tomorrow.' He was already stepping back from the side of the bed. 'Did you hear me? I won't be back tonight. I'm sorry, just a mistake.'

He stepped towards me again and kissed me briefly on the lips. All I saw was the overnight bag in his hand, my overnight bag with the white Laura Ashley pattern just picking up what must have been the beginning of grey dawn light penetrating the white curtains.

A kiss, and he was gone. Quickly, as if I might say something to prevent him from leaving.

I heard the front door close. I didn't go back to sleep. A small hard core of doubt had sprung to life. I lay there, as if to get out of bed, start the day, would bring something unthinkable. There was no reason to doubt, he had made this trip many times, but always in a day, and this time he had made a mistake, except he never made this sort of mistake. He would have spent ages searching for the cheapest deal. Perhaps that was it, he had failed to register that the cheapest deal meant staying overnight, which would not be the cheapest at all because he would have to pay for a hotel, probably the one we always stayed at on the way home from the French house, our last night in France, near Calais, and a favourite restaurant.

Restless, too restless. The doubt was also there, growing and growing, illogical, unwanted. I got up, went through the routine of getting ready for the day, but on automatic pilot, my whole being was taken over by the doubt. Then it would clear for a moment or two, and everything would be fine, as usual. Don't be silly.

But silly, I was going to be. He must have left before 6am. Downstairs I made coffee, in the way he always insisted, heating up what remained from last night, too wasteful to tip it down the sink. The coffee never tasted that good, but I was used to it, heating it up in the microwave, then adding some fresh on top.

Coffee, crossword, cigarettes, the Today programme. I folded the back page of the Telegraph and stared at the first cryptic clue – for quite a long time and seeing nothing there. The radio was just a noise.

I dialled his mobile at 9.30. Dialled again at a quarter to ten, then kept dialling until he answered, and I said it, 'Are you playing away?' Just like that.

'Of course not.' He sounded annoyed.

I could tell he was still in the car. He should have been on the ferry by now.

'Where are you?'

'Held up in traffic.' Then a woman's voice, in the car.

'Who's that?'

'The satnav. You're paranoid.'

'I want you to come home tonight.'

'I told you, I made a mistake with the booking. I'll be home tomorrow. Have a good day.' Click.

That day was to have been a bit different. Weeks ago, I had told him that I would be away for the night, in Berlin, a press trip. And he had said that he would go to Calais that day, on a booze shopping spree, stocking up with wine and brandy to last a couple of months or so. But the press trip had been cancelled.

'I think I'll go anyway,' he'd said. Think about it, a day trip, one he often did while I was at work, coming back in time for a late supper together. What difference did it make that I was supposed to be away?

'We'll never really trust each other,' we had said, more than thirty years earlier when we had left our partners to be together; how could we, when we had each proved so untrustworthy to those innocent parties?

Did I go to work that day? I suppose so, but I can't remember. I think I must have, how else could I have got through the hours till evening. I had said I wanted him to come home tonight. I had said it in a way that made it important.

I don't think I prepared supper. Once more, I called his mobile. It was switched off. I tried to watch television, but turned it off. I didn't call him again. At 3am I sent a text, 'You're a liar and you've ruined everything.'

'Everything' was a passionate affair which had been the first and only for me, but not for him, who had started out by saying that this sort of thing was okay as long as the woman didn't get silly. I should have run then.

I didn't get silly. He did. Told his wife about us, told me that we had fallen in love. I'm not sure I had then, but I was not in love with my husband, had thought about leaving him, going it alone; it was easier to go with someone else, even if I was not sure.

Then ten years of passion and fighting, as if he needed the latter to engender the former, but which I found bewildering and upsetting, and somewhere in between, the being in love had happened, big time. There is no explanation.

'You're a liar and you've ruined everything.' I should not have sent it. I could have pretended that all was as normal, buried the doubt and carried on with my happy, comfortable life. Could I?

Sleep won't come when you most need it. You are flailing about forever just out of reach of that ferry lifebelt which could save you from the paranoia for an hour or so, keep you floating on the reality which is your life as you have made it and believed it would always be.

I must have gone to work the next day because even though I don't remember what I did during the working hours, I can't forget the next bit, 'Do you think we could have a quick drink after work? I want to talk to you about something.'

I have a friend to whom I can say most things, and he to me. Colleagues, friends. The pub is quiet. I tell him the story. He listens and then laughs. He says he thinks it is sweet that a couple who have been together so long can have such a story. Am I being paranoid?

He laughs again. I feel better.

Then I remember that the man I love once gave me VD, in those first ten years, and told me it must have been something he had picked up years earlier when he was in the army in Germany, and I'd bought it, as we do when it's a more convenient choice.

This man who has given me a sleepless night is approaching seventy but I have looked after him well and he looks no more than sixty. He is tall and attractive, even with no hair. He is a prize to hold onto. The life we have made together is a prize to hold onto, especially as there have been such bad times. The good, it seemed, were here to stay, those sunny uplands they talk about; the relationship, the still being in love, and all the rest of it, the children, the grandchildren, the beautiful house and grounds, at last, a successful business. 'You're a liar and you've ruined everything'. I had ruined everything by sending that text.

I had thought he might be home by the time I got back from work, but the house was empty save for the cats, the sweet one and the horrid one who yowled all the time because he was in a permanent bad mood about being a cat. I gave them their supper, which quietened the yowling for a bit.

The only time I had seen my husband cry was when the previous cat had died, this big man with his face all red and puffy. I didn't cry over animals dying, just felt a hole in my life and a concentration of sadness in it. I didn't cry, not anymore. I had in those first ten years, with misery and frustration at his need to argue and mine not to. And then it had stopped. No more arguing, no more crying. What a relief.

Feeling better somehow persisted throughout the evening, and shortly before midnight, I heard him come in. Was it like waiting to find out whether you had passed a vital exam? I think I was nervous. Perhaps the arguing would start again.

I was sitting in the drawing room, knitting. There is great comfort in knitting, making something where there has been nothing. Click, click, clickety-click.

'Hello.'

'Terrible traffic.'

'And at this time of year. Would you like some coffee?'

'I'll get it.'

'It's alright, you're tired.'

Then, back with the coffee.

The heating had gone off, and the room had a chill developing.

'How did it go?'

'Fine.'

'I asked you to come home last night.'

'I couldn't. The ticket mix up.'

I wanted to say that he knew me well enough to have understood that he should have come home, that it had mattered, that he would have managed to do so if he had wanted to, that he must have known it was important.

'Look, I'm sorry I worried you, darling.'

'I tried to call you last night.'

'There was something wrong with my phone.'

Did he get the text?

He had left the room, returning a moment later with a two hundred pack of Silk Cut, but the wrong kind, those extra-long ones that don't taste the same. I didn't say anything, just thanked him, and in another part of my brain registered that he had never before bought me cigarettes. What level of guilt did they represent?

Then we were sitting together and talking and then laughing about the other woman who was satnav, and the sunny uplands were in view again.

I was, of course, exhausted, and I would now be able to sleep. Something had happened but not happened. I went upstairs and was suddenly engulfed by an enormous sense of relief. Thank god, I said to myself, maybe out loud. Thank god I was paranoid and that he was still mine.

Chapter Two

My grandmother taught me to knit. She knitted whole suits for herself while carrying on thoughtful conversations and telling me the stories I loved to hear. She had been engaged to somebody else before she married my grandfather. 'I liked his position but not his disposition, whereas I didn't like your grandfather's position but I liked his disposition.' I think she had said it a lot.

After she died, my grandfather had told me how she had displayed a passion for him that was beyond her strength when she was in her eighties, she had told him she wished she'd loved him as much when they were young as she did now. I thought there was something slightly wrong with this, but I was much younger then.

I didn't like Nick when I first met him. I walked into his office, he was standing by the window, tall, well-built but not overweight, he was wearing a grey suit that had a slight shine to it. Later I saw his shoes, highly polished, extended by a rounded point; I didn't like men who wore fancy footwear, it said a lot about them which played to my young prejudice and intolerance. Later still I was to find that he wore a gold chain. It all added up.

He did his best to charm me, automatic for him on first meeting any woman; but I was wary, having no high opinion of myself. I had been dowdy for some time, way below the radar of any predatory male.

There was no money for new clothes and I didn't want them anyway, nothing interesting would fit me after pregnancy, my shape yet to be fully restored. I tried not to think about it in case it never was.

I had found someone who would look after the baby for a few hours a week and the idea was that I would find some work, anything to stop me from going mad as a mother unsuited to the role.

Nick sat down behind an intimidatingly large desk, indicating that I should take the chair in front of it. This was not going to be the sort of work I wanted to do and I could feel the likelihood of saying the wrong thing because I would not be able to stop myself.

The office was too small for the desk, and for this somehow overbearing man, who had an odd way of speaking, he was trying to sound posher than he was, but he dropped his 'g's.

'Where else have you been workin?' 'This job is mainly writin.'

The door opened and a short fat man blustered in: 'Sorry to interrupto, matey, but I need a word.' He glanced at me, smiled, returned his attention to Nick, who stood up and followed him out of the room.

'A word' turned into an essay. I took in the neatness of everything on the desk, there was a photograph of two children, pre-school, another of a young woman with long blonde hair. It crossed my mind that I should go, I think I wanted to, the man, Nick, was disturbing in a way I could not fathom.

But I waited, and when he returned he was apologetic but there was preoccupation about him, so

I suggested I should leave. Okay, he seemed relieved. He would be in touch. I doubted it.

The week after Nick's booze trip to France, I took a day off and went to London to buy his Christmas present. Shoes, he loved shoes. I had arranged to meet our daughter early evening for a drink and catch-up.

It was a clear, sunny day and I was still basking in the relief of my paranoia having turned out to be just that. And I like shopping, a guilty pleasure, although why should it be guilty? And not today, because I was buying for my husband, not for me. I went to Selfridges where there is a magnificent shoe department. I spent a long time trying to decide on the right pair and was pleased with my choice. It might sound odd, buying shoes for somebody else, who is not there, but I knew Nick's feet as well as I did my own and I had never got it wrong in the past. I bought socks too, then headed for the bar where my daughter and I had arranged to meet at six.

It was down an alleyway not far from Bond Street, narrow, Dickensian, with tables outside under small umbrellas and heaters ranged along the walls either side. There were rugs to put round shoulders, over knees, candles were already lit on the tables.

I found a place with two chairs and settled to do a bit of people-watching as I waited for my daughter. Young women as smart as the pages of Vogue, men in suits, men in leather, waiters and waitresses who looked as if this was not going to be their only career.

And then I saw Sophie, my gorgeous Sophie, as

tall as me and size zero, I always looked to see if other people were noticing her, and they always did, just as she was always late, like her father.

We kissed and one of the waitresses who had a different career up her sleeve came by for our order. Sophie wanted a glass of Chablis, so I ordered a bottle, why not? It was nearly Christmas. Life was good.

And Sophie was on good form, telling her wonderful stories about life in London, she was made for London and made the most of it.

I loved listening to her, hearing her happiness, watching her beautiful face, the porcelain doll skin which didn't really need make-up but had plenty, applied with great care. Sophie, plump as a child, took nothing for granted now that she had turned into this other creature.

Her boyfriend Tom had a new job, so we talked about this for a bit and the new flat they shared in Hackney. I liked Tom, he was everything Sophie needed after his disastrous predecessor who had dumped her by text after six years together. 'I'm in it for the long haul,' that boy had said to me a few months before the text, as if the relationship was to be endured. He was clever, but not in the rounded way of Tom. He was a medical student who thought he wanted to be a musician but had followed his parents into the profession and chose to resent them for it. He was resentful and jealous and thrashed about for an adequate reason to have such a chip on his shoulder. They had met while still at school and Sophie had gone with him to a university that did medicine and where she did politics and where he guarded her with his jealous chip.

It was good to see her happy now. The waitress came and poured more wine, hurrying us towards the next bottle. The smell of something savoury and delicious wafted into the alley. Nick had told me to come back as late as I liked, to have a nice time with Sophie, perhaps she would have supper with me.

There was a brief lull, Sophie catching her breath in between stories. I thought I would tell her about my stupid paranoia, how I had jumped to the conclusion that satnav was another woman, it seemed like a funny little anecdote worthy of sharing, just to make her laugh. Then she wanted to see the shoes. She liked them, and the socks, they would be a joint present from both of us.

Then she was telling me about a woman at work who was paranoid, and then I was telling her the story.

I didn't finish it. Sophie was crying. Where did this come from? What is it? What is it?

Later, I wondered how things might have been had I not started that story. It's difficult not to have the 'what if's.

In the summer, Sophie had been home for a while, before she and Tom got it together, while she was still dealing with her own 'what if's. She had come in from the garden and her father was on the phone, speaking, she told me, in a way he would talk to her or her sister, or me. He had not finished the call when he saw that she was there. She went into the kitchen to try and avoid hearing any more because she had heard enough to realise the unthinkable.

I don't want to give the impression that she cries a lot because she doesn't, and usually, thank goodness, out of extreme frustration rather than misery. She was crying when Nick found her in the kitchen after he had finished the call. I don't know exactly what was said, but it turned into an argument, as was so often the case between them. What I remember her telling me was his final salvo, 'What are you going to do about it?' said in a careless, throwaway manner, as if it didn't really matter to him.

'He bought me cigarettes. He's never done that before,' I said. Guilt, or perhaps no longer caring if I smoked myself to death. Both. Oh, for goodness sake! Don't think like a victim. Don't be a victim, it doesn't have to be like this. There must be an explanation. There must be.

These staccato thoughts were being held inside, while outwardly I had to be a mother comforting the distressed child. I was super-calm, for me the best fall-back position for any emergency; be calm and measured and nothing can be as bad as it might seem.

'Do you remember that time Tom and I were staying the weekend at home and I'd cooked that vodka fish dish and made crème brulee, and dad wasn't back from wherever he was, and it was getting so late?'

'I thought you were upset because the food was spoiling.' I said this in that slightly distracted and resigned way that comes with new knowledge.

Sophie didn't need to say any more, and I didn't ask if Tom had known. I had yet to start thinking of myself as the ignorant, pitiable person that I must have been.

'I think it was the satnav,' I said, 'that I heard.' But it was taking me in the right direction. Sophie said nothing.

I looked around at the people at other tables, chattering away, oblivious of course. If they had seen Sophie crying, they had lost interest. A sense of detachment had quickly developed in me, or perhaps a numbness, like a bad wound can be before the real pain sets in. Did I wish I had not told Sophie the story? Yes, and no.

For some reason that seemed necessary at the time, I promised her that I would talk to her father when I got home and that I would let her know, and with a sense of dread purpose, we parted, hugging and kissing. We both knew the truth now, even if I had yet to accept it.

I took a taxi to King's Cross and seem to remember talking banalities to the driver, what else was there to do? There was a train about to leave and I ran for it, even though I would have preferred to miss it; but I needed to know now, to have him tell me it was all in my imagination, that we were fine.

On the train, the calm part of me considered the options, with say nothing the favourite. Say nothing and there might be nothing. Say nothing and if there was something, it might just go away. My first husband had taken that line, but it had not worked for him. When you know, you know, even if you don't want to believe.

I've always been impulsive, going off with Nick was impulsive but also irresistible, and didn't even seem wrong at the time. Impulse made me send him a text from the train, asking him to pick me up from the station, adding that we needed to talk.

How do you get through those long moments just before everything might change, and not for the better? I don't know how I endured that train journey. At best, I thought, it would turn out to be no more than a fling, Nick and I had something special. It had taken years to get right, to live in harmony, which, surely, was what any couple wanted after so long together. And I was still in love with him, more so than ever. I loved everything about him, his smell, his touch, the fact that he was mine. I couldn't lose him. It was unthinkable.

Thank god there had been no one I knew on the train because I might have been rude to them by not wanting to talk. I was counting small blessings, like displacement thoughts, but when the train drew into my station I left my seat with an awful weariness, the stuffing had been knocked out of me good and proper, and the deciding round was yet to come. Did I think in that way?

Nick was waiting in the car. I do remember that it was raining and windy. I got in as if everything was normal. He asked about Sophie and had we had a nice time together, and I answered as expected, but without elaborating, that just wasn't possible.

It took less than five minutes to get home. I dashed in through the rain and so that I could get in the house first and hide the shoes, the Christmas present. I wanted them to be a surprise. The socks I would put in his stocking, along with chocolates and peppermints and cologne, and a walnut and satsuma. When Sophie was still at home, she would come into our bedroom on Christmas morning and the three of us would open our stockings, the time when it was just the three of us, before the rest of the family arrived for the huge meal and then the games played only at Christmas.

Having hidden the shoes upstairs, I came down and found Nick at the back door, clearing away leaves, which kept blowing back and were now encroaching into the hallway. What on earth was he doing? He seemed distracted and at the same time as if at any moment, he might lose his temper.

'We need to talk.' There, no longer just a text, I'd said it. A cliché, but what else?

'Damn leaves.'

Chapter Three

There was a long-running correspondence in the Telegraph one year about how many leaves were shed by an oak tree. I think it was oak. There were lots of mathematical suggestions, and I suppose that would be the only way, other than counting them, and that would surely send you mad.

We had a beech, a massive one close to our bedroom, its branches yearning to cover the roof. There was an owl in it one year, I loved that. The leaves, I dare say, were as numerous as those from an oak. They took a lot of clearing up.

I fetched a cup of coffee. Nick already had one, but still, he had not come to join me in the drawing room. Possibilities kept presenting themselves, I could go to bed, avoid the 'we need to talk'; I could go out and help him with the leaves, but I kind of thought he would give up on them if I did that, besides, it was bonkers at this time of night, in the rain and the wind. He would have to come in before long.

And he did. At last. But still the displacement activities (what would we do without them), his coffee was cold, he went out to the kitchen for a refill, spent a bit of time fiddling with the dishwasher, I could hear everything with a sharp clarity.

When he could think of nothing else to avoid talking to me, he came back and sat down, tried to drink the coffee, which must have been too hot. He stared into the steaming cup, leaning forward, very still, as if trying to make up his mind about something. I too was very still, waiting, watching, withering inside.

He spoke first. 'Alright, I am having an affair.' The emphasis was on 'am'.

That terrible calm came over me, confirmation of the worst, a slight fuzz in my head.

'Who is it? Someone I know?'

'No, you don't know her. She's someone who works at one of the suppliers we deal with.' He said this quickly, as if it was none of my business, an edge of impatience.

'How long?'

'Oh, years, I should think.'

'Don't.'

'Since February.'

'But why?'

'I don't know, it's just one of those things.'

One of those things …

'You took her to France.'

'I knew I'd have to tell you. You were so upset last week.'

'You said I was paranoid.'

He shrugged.

'That time you were so late back, when Sophie and Tom were here.'

'Sophie knew. She chose not to say anything.'

'How awful it must have been for her.'

Another shrug. He didn't care. The imperative was elsewhere.

'I want to talk to this woman.'

'You can't. Her husband doesn't know. I don't

want to put her in an awkward position.'

'You don't want to put her in an awkward position! You must give her up. End it.'

'I don't think I can.'

'Of course you can!'

'I'm very taken with her.'

'You mean you've fallen in love with her?'

'I think it's possible to love two people at the same time.'

Did this give me hope? I was rapidly moving towards a willingness to compromise, to hold on no matter what.

'Where do you meet?' I don't know why I asked that. Did it matter? But I was overcome by a need to know everything.

'Hotels. I get a special deal.'

'You just go there and have sex, and then leave?'

'Yes.'

'You've never bought me cigarettes before.'

'They were on special offer.'

'What did you buy her?'

'Belgian chocolates. She likes Belgian chocolates.'

'You must call, tell her that I know.' It might be possible that my knowing would see her off, that the situation would seem too dangerous for her to let it continue.

'I'll text her. I can't put her situation in jeopardy.'

'But she's put herself in jeopardy by having an affair. How old is she? What's she like?'

'She's much younger than me, but not that young. She has a wonderful body, it looks thirty years younger than it is. And she loves sex. D'you know, she had not had sex for twenty years. Her husband has a serious heart condition.' He was rattling on now, as if it was a relief, which probably it was, to be saying all this.

'Have you bought her a Christmas present?'

'Yes.'

'What is it?'

'She said she wanted a ring.'

'But when is she going to wear it?'

'When she's with me.'

'Was it expensive? Did you get it from that shop we always go to in Calais?' It was like picking at a wound, unable to leave it alone.

'Well, it's such good value there.'

'I have to call Sophie. I promised I would.'

I didn't call, she did. 'It's true. Since February.'

And Sophie called her sister and she immediately called me, and then Vicky was in the house. Nick had retreated to the study. Vicky flung open the door: 'What have you done!'

She slammed the door shut and I could hear her raised voice, berating her step-father. Vicky very rarely lost her cool, but when she did...

She was genuinely concerned for me, but what could be done? It was already done. And it was very late. Vicky had to get back to her family and be up early. Sophie, tearful at the other end of the phone, had to be reassured that things would be sorted out. Being sensible was the thing, even if it was the last thing I felt like being. I should have raged and told Nick to get out. I think I should have hit him. He might have hit me back. A physical pain might have numbed the other for a moment.

Nothing like this happened. We went to bed, I was always under the covers before him. When he came through from the bathroom, he was tiptoeing, as if trying not to wake me, as if he could possibly believe that I would be asleep.

In bed, he reached for my hand. 'Are you alright, darling?'

'What do you think?'

We lay there like those supine stone statues that lie on tombs. Except they don't snore. Incredibly, Nick had fallen asleep, perhaps at ease now that it was all out in the open. I got up and went to Sophie's old room. It might have struck me that I would never again share a bed with Nick, but I don't think it did, not that night.

I didn't sleep. Thoughts went round and round, like dirty washing in the machine. The cruelty of a night unslept making time stand still.

When dawn broke, I lay there looking at Sophie's things, the posters on the walls, the soft toys stacked on top of her bookcase, the childhood books still lined up, discarded handbags in a heap to the side of the bed. Stuff everywhere, Sophie held on to everything. Brief moments impinged, the time we were in San Francisco, the three of us in a hotel room, Nick in his Mr Hyde persona, insisting on a row about nothing. Me, jetlagged from having flown from London to meet them, exasperated, shutting myself in the bathroom to escape. Sophie, still a child, hammering on the door, coming in, upset.

'I don't know how much more of this I can take,' I had said, not to her, to myself.

'No! No! You're the two people I love most in the world. No!'

Why did he do this, the switching personalities? Even his eyes looked different when he was Hyde. They narrowed and developed a spark. Spiteful words ensued. Unnecessary, un-called-for venom, a process which would shift onto Sophie before long, if it had not already. It had been like that for years with me, his need to fight, and always over nothing at all, escalating into real nastiness, things said which could not be erased. Did I fight back? Of course, but the difference was I did not enjoy it, it upset and bewildered me.

We met in the bathroom on day one of the rest of my life. He'd had a shower, and a bath sheet was wrapped around his waist. While he stood in front of the mirror, trimming his beard, I sat in the Lloyd loom chair, the one that had come from my grandparents' home, and watched him.

We started talking. I think he asked if I had slept well. He was unreachable.

What were we going to do? That had to be the question. But I asked another.

'Have you spoken to her?'

'Yes.'

'What did she say?'

'She says she wants to carry on dating.'

This should have made me terribly angry, but anger had yet to come.

'And her husband?'

'He doesn't know. And she doesn't want her daughter to know either.'

'How old is her daughter?'

'The same age as Sophie.'

Throughout this exchange he continued fussing with his beard, looking at his own face rather than mine.

Then he stopped and did turn to face me.

'Women just throw themselves at me, you know.'

He was serious, and he was speaking to me as if I was his confidante.

'Where do we go from here?' I asked, as much to myself as to him.

'I don't know.'

'You won't give her up?'

'I told you, I don't think I can.'

'What if her husband finds out?'

'I'd have to look after her. Find her somewhere to live. I couldn't let her down.'

The enormous injustice of this should have hit me harder, but the blows were coming so thick and fast.

I heard myself say, 'An open marriage, then?'

'Yes, an open marriage.'

How ridiculous of me to take a crumb of comfort from this.

He had moved through to the dressing room now, and I followed.

'How will you feel when I take advantage of it being open?'

'I won't like it,' he said, without pause.

Chapter Four

If your husband dies, you don't go to work the next day, probably not for a couple of weeks or so.

I drove to the office without being aware of anything I passed on the journey. I went to my desk, switched on my computer, made myself a coffee, blessed routine.

Tony, my colleague, who sat opposite, came in, cheery, always cheery. Then he paused and was looking at me.

'It wasn't paranoia,' was all I said.

'Come on, let's go out to the fag shed.'

'Later.' I wanted to get on, to go through my emails, to have something else to think about, but within the hour I had retreated to the shed, and Tony came too.

I told him what had happened and he said he couldn't believe it. I said I couldn't either, but that I had to.

I picked out all the worst bits, him saying that women threw themselves at him, him saying he couldn't let HER down, couldn't upset her apple cart.

How I got through that day I can't think, I don't remember much of it, anything that happened quickly overshadowed when I got home that night and the compulsive process of unravelling it all took hold of me.

I made supper for us. When I had come in, he was still in the study, he worked from home, and was at his desk when I left in the mornings and still there until supper was on the table. It was going to be the same tonight, as if the routine could contradict the upheaval.

The table laid, candle lit, as it always was for supper, he came through when I called to him that it was ready.

He sat down at the head of the table, me to one side. I helped him to the food and immediately he began to eat, as if all was normal. I looked at the food on my plate and knew I would not be able to stomach it. I sipped at my glass of wine. What I wanted was a cigarette.

He didn't ask me what sort of a day I'd had, but then he never did. The only thing that was different tonight was not having the telly on. He didn't want to continue the morning's conversation, I could tell, but he must have known it was inevitable.

He finished his meal, declined a second helping, and began to clear up. This was how we were, I cooked, he cleared up, made the coffee.

All of this he did, while I took my glass of wine into the drawing room and waited.

He seemed to take an exceptionally long time in the kitchen, although it was probably no longer than usual.

At last he joined me, bringing in the coffee on a tray. Neither of us was going to switch on the television, and when the silence could endure no longer, he asked me again if I was alright.

'You want me to be like Mrs Clark,' I said.

He liked this. Mrs Clark, wife of Alan Clark, notorious womaniser, who had even taken his girlfriend on their honeymoon. Mrs Clark, who had put up with it over decades and remained Mrs Clark, who, it was generally acknowledged, Alan had loved, he was simply incapable of fidelity. Mrs Clark, who once on television had described her husband as an 'S' 'H' 'one' 'T'.

'Yes, Mrs Clark,' he said, with something like satisfaction.

Then he stood up. Began to pace the room, which was long and a little too narrow.

'I think at our time of life we have to be pragmatic,' he was saying. 'We can live like brother and sister, friends. You will sleep in the spare room.'

'Have you ever brought her here?'

'Once. She wanted to see the house. We didn't stay long.'

'Did you, in our bed?'

'I can't remember.'

I knew this meant that they had. How much worse could it get? Had she looked through my things? What other violations were there?

'What's she like? You haven't told me what she's like.'

'She's Asian. She's exotic.'

'What sort of Asian? Indian?'

'Filipino.'

'She doesn't work for one of our suppliers, does she? How did you meet her?'

'She does!'

'Tell me the truth. I need to know the truth.' I knew this would be hard for him. Nick told lies but always justified their telling to himself, and occasionally to me.

'Online.'

'But you're married,' I said, stupidly. 'How? Which site? Where?'

'Illicit Encounters.'

Another moment to freeze. At work I was regularly sent emails from this site, I was just a random recipient who worked on a newspaper. They sent me press releases which were clever and funny and which I had forwarded to Nick to make him laugh.

'How many?'

'What?'

'Women have you met.'

'Some of them were terrible, not at all like the pictures they posted. They were really grot. There was one woman who was alright, but she wanted someone to go away with for weekends, and I couldn't do that. I told her she was on the wrong dating site.'

'Where did you meet them?'

'In a hotel in Huntingdon.' He said the name and immediately I pictured him there, in the lounge, meeting a woman he had never met before and with whom he would be trying to decide whether to have sex.

'How do you see their pictures? They can't post them on the site?'

'You read their profile and if you like it and they like yours, you send each other pictures by post. You can have a PO Box.'

'What does she really do, this exotic Filipino?' I

knew there was an edge to the way I said this that he would not like.

'Marketing, but I can't say more than that. She told me not to.'

'For goodness sake!'

I suppose it would have gone on in this fruitless vein, but the doorbell did its throttled buzz. Nick would normally go to the door at night, but he didn't move, perhaps he guessed it would be Vicky, and by the time she was up the stairs and into the hallway, he was again in the study, the door closed.

Vicky had grown up with Nick, but he was not her father. Her concern was only for me, and for her baby sister, with whom she had been in constant touch since the news broke. Sophie called Vicky's mobile while we were sitting there, and I could hear her sobbing.

'I just don't understand why this has happened,' I was saying quietly. 'I thought we were happy.'

Vicky stayed, reluctant to leave me but with her own life tugging at her and Nick making no appearance. It was late when she went and he emerged.

'I don't know why there is such a fuss. Thousands of people do this all the time.' He said this as if talking about something we were observing rather than it being the end of us.

'Why did you?'

He had not sat down, had begun fussing with a gap in the curtains. He didn't want to look at me. 'I suppose I wanted to see what was out there.' He made it sound like an academic exercise. He was distancing himself from the damage he had caused. I think it

might have been then that I realised I would never be
able to reach him again.

Chapter Five

But I did. And I might have wished I hadn't, yet it is impossible not to want to know more and more, to prize out details that can only make it hurt to the point where you find yourself in a masochistic compulsion to hear the very worst.

I didn't have to try that hard. Nick wanted me to know, and not just about her but about me. He was sitting beside me on the sofa. For years and years we had always sat together on the sofa, made love on it, sat close, and then it had stopped. I had bought a large armchair because I liked the way it looked, and Nick emigrated to it, without me really noticing. He would fall asleep in front of the telly and I would sometimes gaze at him and think how glad I was that he was mine. I really did have that thought, many times.

The telly was beside the point now. He sat by me and seemed to be making an attempt to be friendly. He patted my hand and started talking as if to himself.

'You've looked after me for more than thirty years, but the thing is, I think we need different people at different times in our lives. Carys said that.'

'Carys knows?'

Carys was operations manager for the business, a woman whose first husband had left her and she was now married to a good-looking man with no brain.

'You told her.'

'No, of course not, it was just something she said.'

'When? Why? Did you have an affair with her?'

'Oh, she wanted to, but, no, I learnt my lesson long ago about flings with staff.'

And, of course, I had to know who they were. And he told me. Any others? Any of our friends?

Some names were spoken, and I knew before he said them who they would be.

'What's wrong with me?' I thought, but had actually said.

His answer should have been 'nothing' or some such, but instead, he chose to tell me.

'You drink too much, you eat too much. You are too fat and too old to fancy.' He was still patting my hand, like a doctor who had no choice but to deliver the fatal diagnosis. His tone was gentle, as if he was being cruel to be kind, laying the relationship to rest in the only way he knew how.

All his accusations had an element of truth, so I didn't deny them, but I didn't think I was out of control with three of them. Long ago, Nick had made me feel more attractive than I had ever imagined, and that was something he had given me which would not be entirely lost.

For the next few days, we moved around one another with caution. I remembered how during the week of blissful denial, before the meeting with Sophie, we had been in the kitchen, he was at the sink and I had been putting something in a cupboard. I had been moving past him and paused to put my arms around him. He had gone rigid. I had chosen not to think anything of it.

And in the endless cycle of replay that plagued me

at night when I was alone in Sophie's bed, I alighted on other clues I had failed or chosen not to pick up over the past months. His love-making had become careless, even painful, joyless, I suppose, on his part. 'I've got to fuck the fat frump I don't fancy.'

I continued cooking supper each night and not being able to eat it, while his appetite seemed undiminished. I still lit the candle. I sat there while he cleared his plate, accepted a second helping. 'You're not eating much,' he said, as if this was surprising.

I think he thought this might turn into the new normal, like the 'thousands of other people who went through this all the time'. Friday came and I did what I had for some years, went to the pub after work with Tony. We had started doing this because we never had time during the working day and we liked to talk shop. We had tried several pubs before we found The Fountain, where we had got to know the regulars. I would stay for about an hour, have no more than a couple of glasses of wine and then drive home and meet Nick in another pub close by and where Carys and her husband and other people who worked for us would already be well away. Carys had a big mouth anyway and would become increasingly voluble as she oiled it with the night's poison. She said 'fuck' a lot, using the word like strong seasoning for an otherwise bland diet.

There was another clue I had dismissed. A few weeks ago I had arrived at the second pub and found Nick at the bar. There were no spare seats but he remained sitting on one of the high stools and let me order a drink for myself. He seemed to be in one of his moods, so I talked to his side-kick, Jerry, facilities manager for the business and with whom I got on well.

The thing is, I like conversation, but Nick, who is not interested in what other people say and think, had always made me feel as if I was overstepping the line by engaging in interesting chit-chat. Perhaps he resented not being capable of this himself, I don't know, and I doubt he does either. He had once said to me 'You are too friendly with people'. I didn't think so but still felt in the wrong.

But not when I wasn't with him. That hour in the first pub on Friday nights I loved. The regulars included a giant of a man in every sense. Adam was beautiful to look at, a man whose presence was immediately noticed. And he relished conversation.

Half a dozen of us, sometimes more, hardly ever fewer, would sit at one of the big round tables outside, smoking under the heaters, saying what we thought, uninhibited. It was a combination of that end-of-a-hard-week feeling, letting go, talking about the big things in the world.

I was always the first to leave, I had a husband to get back to, and that was fine.

There had been a spark between Adam and me from the start, enjoyed by both of us, giving that extra edge to our conversations about 9/11 conspiracy theories, what should happen in the Middle East, whether women should have Brazilians.

That Friday, Adam saw straight away something had happened to me, although I don't suppose it was that difficult to spot. Tony, who knew, wasn't going to say anything unless I did.

There was only one way to say it, flippantly. Bare facts. And I didn't want pity, I just wanted them to know, the people around the table who I knew only on Friday evenings.

I can't remember what any one of them said, but they were immediately supportive and, naturally enough, enthralled. I told them about satnav, the accusation of paranoia, the week of reprieve, the confession, and being told that I was too old to fancy. I left out the other bits.

I didn't leave after the usual hour was up. I stayed on, drinking three, four glasses of wine. I stayed until the others drifted inside for more warmth, until Tony had gone home and it was just Adam and me. He was being kind, and predatory.

'Be careful,' one of the last remaining regulars murmured to me as we passed through the bar.

Adam's house was a short walk from the pub, there was a long, dark alleyway, the sort of route I would have avoided had I been alone, but it crossed my mind that the way I felt now I would have sought it out. I was surely irreparably damaged already. Bring it on.

'You're free,' Adam said when we reached his house and were taking off our coats. 'You can do whatever you like.'

Until that moment, the prospect of freedom had equated only with loneliness, and the doing whatever I liked ring-fenced by the knowledge that I could no longer do what I really wanted.

Adam's house was dirty and smelly, a man living alone and habituated to making the most of it. There was a huge coffee table between two sofas, on it, a collection of cans and bottles, an ashtray long ago ready to be emptied, packets of tobacco and small parcels of I didn't know what, other than that they contained drugs. 'Be careful' I'd been told, but that was the last thing I felt like being tonight.

Adam rolled a spliff, lit it and with a long, laconic stretch, handed it to me. I took a drag, coughed, took another one. A moment or two later I felt cotton wool invade my brain then start to unravel, lifting me into a mezzanine of momentary escape. My gaze roamed the room, focusing sharply on a grotesque painting which seemed to be depicting blood; then the sharpness dissipating, smothered by the sweet floating sensation, and for the first time in a week, hunger.

But it was no more than a brief sensation, I was not ready to start eating.

The smell of a big man who never opened a window took on a new element. The room danced a little.

'I can't drive home.'

'I'll make up a bed for you.'

Unsteadily, I followed him up the narrow stairs. He was grabbing bedding from a shelf on the landing and ahead of us was another flight, even more narrow, steep and twisting, going up to a room in the roof. Beyond the stairs, his bedroom door was open. I went past him and waited.

He disappeared for a while. I took off my clothes and got into bed. The cliché had happened, I was beyond caring. I was free. I could do whatever I liked.

What did I feel? Gratitude. I had been given a displacement thought, replaying the way Adam had taken me. Fat, too old to fancy, I had spent the night with a man twenty years my junior, a man who was undeniably attractive. I thought I was back on the horse.

I didn't sleep. Very early I left, took in a deep breath from the freshness of the new day. There was no traffic at this hour and I was home before I thought Nick would be up, but he was in the kitchen making coffee.

I greeted him brightly and said nothing about having not come home. He was in a morose mood, and the long-held default position in me flitted towards guilt for having caused it.

'It didn't take you long,' he said, and I knew what he meant.

My response was to offer to make him breakfast.

'You're up early,' I said.

'Don't you remember? I'm going to collect a new car.'

I didn't remember because I had not been told.

'You need to sign the finance form.'

'Okay.'

I had taken my cup of coffee through to the drawing-room and, after a few minutes, he came in with some papers, folded over so only the last page, where I was to sign, could be seen. He held out the pen, and I hesitated. It occurred to me that in recent months this scenario had played out several times, being asked to sign documents I had not read. The foolishness of this struck me now in a way I would never have contemplated a week ago.

'I don't think I can do this.' I had reached out to take the pen but now I was drawing back.

'What do you mean?' he said tetchily.

'I mean, I don't think I should be signing anything, not now,' I heard myself saying. My tone was measured, I had never spoken to him in this way in the past.

'For god's sake, it's only a formality.'

'I can't sign it.'

'You're just doing this to spite me.' He had gone red in the face, a bit puffy. Was I guilty of spite?

He was going on now about everything having been arranged, that the car had to be collected today, that I had to sign. Here was the first real tangible moment of the end game. I could see him wrestling with himself, he always got what he wanted, which once had been me and now was a car. He couldn't bear to lose, he had to find another way.

He retreated to the study and I went upstairs to take a bath, to wash Adam away from my body if not from my mind, to keep that replay going every time I came near to being engulfed by another wave of utter despair.

The girls kept calling me, as if I was in a place of danger. Was I alright? What was I going to do?

What was I going to do? Getting up so early had given me a long day to get through. What was I going to do?

Chapter Six

From the start, I had collaborated with Nick's need to get what he wanted, ignored the warning signs that were going to take me on an awfully long path to a dead end.

'Why are you being like this?' I would say in the early days, bewildered at how charm could so suddenly switch to harsh words and cold disdain.

'Being like what?' would come the sharp riposte. But I could never put it into words, and eventually, it would become "Nickish", which he'd dismiss as me 'being silly'.

He had made a carapace for himself from a young age. His father had died when he was six, a wound to the head from fighting in Italy at the end of the War and which had triggered cancer. His mother, who had died in her fifties from another cancer, had married the first man who asked, someone who had come to do repairs to the house and who was a bully because he knew he could not match her intellect. The first thing he'd done when he moved in was to have Nick's dog put down. But why? Because he could.

I spent most of the day with the girls. Sophie had come from London to be with me and we were all at Vicky's house, where I was allowed to smoke in the circumstances, and a lot of circular discussion took place. The only thing I really took in from that day was not to sign anything.

By late afternoon I wanted my daughters to get on

with their own lives and was also, obtusely, drawn back to take part in the drama in which they should have no part.

In the driveway at home was a new car, a big BMW, the colour I couldn't see, not that it mattered. Our cars were bought on the company and Nick had needed my signature as his co-director. At last, I felt angry. I hurried into the house to find him. He wasn't downstairs. Somehow, I couldn't bring myself to call out his name.

He was upstairs in the spare bedroom where I did the ironing, and which he was doing now, with excessive concentration. His face was already infused with that red puffiness which always gave him away in a lie.

'How did you get the car?' I asked, the measured tone still there.

'I signed for it as a sole trader.' He'd rehearsed this. 'I have taken you off the company as a director.' I was sure he couldn't do this but was not sufficiently sure of my ground to protest; besides, I had known even as I first saw the car, that he must have forged my signature. There again, if he had done so now, why not all those times he had me signing things over the past months? He hadn't needed to, I had been happy to sign whatever he put in front of me.

I retreated downstairs, too angry and frustrated to stay in the same room with him; but he followed me, even though it seemed he had nothing more to say. I sat down in the drawing room and tried to think what to do next. I felt a sudden physical loathing towards him, with his liar's face and for having the capacity to destroy me.

'Oh, why can't you leave me alone,' I almost begged him, but I could hear the anger as well.

'I've as much right to be here as you have,' he said, like another rehearsed line.

'Oh, why don't you just fuck off,' I said, as he loomed behind where I was sitting.

'How dare you be so rude to me.' My god, he sounded genuinely insulted. It was rare for me to use four-letter words, and when I did, I felt uncomfortable. How dare he make me resort to one, and yet I felt rightly rebuked. It was a long time since there had been harsh words between us and I'd thought that was good but now I began to see that harmony bored Nick. For the first time I wondered when he had stopped loving me, and the awful realisation came that it was probably years.

He had now left the room. Random memories came into play. I saw the chair he had thrown across the room in a fit of jealous frustration when I had told him I was going to be away for a night, and remembered the passion, now transferred to someone else. That had been such a long time ago, the angry passion, and I hadn't even missed it; I'd been thankful for the arrival of harmony.

What was I going to do? I would have to leave. I'd never get him to go. The false calm had returned when he came back into the room with a tray of coffee. He sat down next to me and took my hand.

'You're not going to give her up, are you?'

'No.'

'I'm going to move out. I'll go for six months. I need time to think.'

'Where will you go?'

'I'll think of somewhere.' It occurred to me that I didn't have enough money.

He sighed. 'I think if you go, you may never come back.'

'I'll need some money.'

'How much?'

'I'll find somewhere to rent in Cambridge.'

'Can't you stay with Vicky?' Everything he said made it worse because he wasn't trying to stop me.

It was late, but I phoned a friend in Cambridge and asked her if I could come and stay, remaining where I was felt like being a pariah at a party, each exchange with Nick taking another piece of self-respect from me. I had yet to think in terms of survival, but one thing I had to sort out quickly was sleep, it just wasn't happening and my mind had developed a sort of jetlag-type altered state.

In brief staccato sentences, I told Julie what had happened, and straightaway she said: 'My house is your house.' I left that night.

Inevitably, we stayed up late, Julie listening, me talking, when it was usually the other way round. Julie was the sort of person who lit up a room, everyone loved her in the way such people are loved, we are greedy for their company. She lived alone in a Victorian terraced house in the city, close to the river. Her home was a cocoon of bohemian fabric, drapes and throws flung over deep sofas in front of an open fire she had stoked up from dying embers. It glowed brightly now and drew the eye as I recounted and recounted.

'You'll have to get him back.'

Yes, I thought, but said I didn't think so.

'Nick is an attractive man.' She seemed to be implying that I had been careless to let him go, that if I put my mind to it, all could be retrieved. And then, as if changing her mind, she said a woman we both knew was leaving Cambridge and letting her house, just around the corner.

'I'll call her.'

'But it's late.'

'Oh, she won't mind.'

I thought she would, but Julie was already picking up her phone, and I didn't protest.

Early the next morning, we walked the short distance to view the house, a smaller version of Julie's, but perfectly adequate. After the inspection, the three of us stood in what passed for a dining room and the woman, Laura, paused and peered at me.

'Are you sure you are not going to get back together?' She wanted to know from the point of view of a landlady, which was not unreasonable. I suppose I was not ready to be sure, but the bridges were burning.

The brief stagnation was over. I went to the doctor, the doctor I had known for thirty years. At last, I cried, something I had not done since the early years of the marriage when frustration would drive me to tears as Nick went full throttle into Mr Hyde. I had always found tears shameful, something I didn't really do, yet now I felt uninhibited in shedding them into the tissues the doctor was handing to me. Uninhibited or just lost?

I seemed to have been with the doctor a lot longer than the appointment allowed and began to feel pariahish again.

'There are people in the waiting room who are really sick,' I heard myself saying. 'Some of them may have life-threatening conditions.'

'This is life-threatening.'

Such a thought had not occurred to me. What did he think I was going to do?

Pills were prescribed, lots of them, and he gave me the name of a counsellor. I took it, but could not imagine myself going to see her. Counsellors were for other people, those who couldn't cope. I didn't see it then, but I had not even begun to cope, other than resorting to drugs and removing myself from the scene of my paltry little drama. As Nick had said, thousands of people did what he had, all the time.

I did sleep that night. Julie's spare bed was wonderfully comfortable and the pills knocked me out almost straight away. Julie was going away the next day, off to France, where she made frequent visits to see old friends from the years she had spent there with her lover. It was going to be a couple of weeks before I could move into Laura's house, but the living alone was going to start now.

'I don't want to live alone,' I had said to Nick.

'Neither do I,' he had said.

Chapter Seven

We arranged to meet at a pub in the city. I suggested a place where there were old leather sofas outside in a covered courtyard with heaters and ashtrays. The plan was to talk further about Mrs Clark.

Nick was always late, and always in a temper about being so, blaming traffic, even when there wasn't any. I ignored this preamble. I might have wanted to tell him that he had not allowed enough time, that he never did, but there was no point.

Settled with drinks, sitting together on the low, worn-out sofa, heater on and no one else there in the dead of winter, we skirted around how the conversation would begin. We had been to this pub before, a birthday party, and we had sat out here, it had been only a few months ago. The unimaginable change.

'I've got the things you asked for. They're in the car.' What had I asked for? I couldn't think. My face must have looked blank.

'The clothes you asked for.'

'Oh, yes.'

My mind went back more than thirty years to another pub, the two of us meeting there because we had just become lovers and everything was still in the moment, and we had not known what to say.

Three decades in which perhaps we should have talked more than we did, rather than making assumptions. I didn't know if Nick had any now, I certainly had none. I was being open-minded only for the sake of survival.

We took small, careful sips from our drinks, and waited. Another couple came out and sat closer to us than they might. We remained silent, and then Nick leaned closer to me and said, 'I don't know what to do'. He rubbed his hand over his face and then added, 'She won't leave her husband.'

'I don't think I can be second best,' I heard myself say.

He did not respond. How could he, to that?

'Mrs Clark,' I said after a pause. It was like raising a point on an agenda.

'What do you think?'

'I don't know. I feel I have lost everything, my husband, lover, best friend, my home, everything.'

'I suppose we could try it,' he said, flatly. At the same time, I could see that he was in turmoil, and I saw hope in this.

The other couple were still there, so I suggested we go back to Julie's. 'We'll be alone, she's gone to France.'

A cold wind was gusting into our faces as we left our unfinished drinks and went to the car park. He followed me through the town and when we got to Julie's road, it had started to rain. It was a miserable night.

'It's incredibly good of Julie to let you stay,' he said, and, again, I wondered how his mind was working. Did he see our situation as being in limbo?

When we were first together, there had been one

occasion when he had gone to see his wife, and my husband had come to see me, and all the possibilities were still there. Later, I discovered that he had gone to bed with her, to see if he could go back; perhaps now I was thinking along the same lines but with a different outcome.

We were sitting in front of an unlit fire, he seemed to have folded into himself, his hands covering his face. I touched his arm, he flinched: 'I can't betray her.'

'But, I'm your wife.'

'I'm so torn,' he said, heartfelt, still not showing me his face.

I waited. It seemed like a pivotal moment. Then he stood up and said he had to go to the loo. He went upstairs and I heard him trip on the step that went down into the bathroom. He was up there a long time and eventually I went up, to find him in the open doorway attempting to mend the light pull, trying to re-attach the cord to the ceiling switch, cursing.

'Bloody stupid thing.'

'Let me do it.' I knew how, it had happened before, but he wanted to persist.

'Leave it. Please leave it.'

He followed me downstairs and perhaps we both knew the moment, if there'd been one, had passed.

'I ought to go.'

'Yes.'

I followed him to the door, where he remembered the clothes he had brought for me, went to his car and fetched them in, now cursing the rain.

'Shall we meet again next week?' I said, thinking that he was not ready to let me go.

'If you want to.'

'This is awful.'

He dumped the clothes in the hallway and then turned and kissed me on the cheek.

'Am I still your darling?' Why did I say that? Why did he say "yes"?'

We met the following week and this time had supper in the sofa pub. However, my appetite was still zero, while his remained unaffected. We were more business-like about Mrs Clark and seemed to reach some sort of accommodation in much the same way the real Mrs Clark must have done; if we were to pursue this plan, the new way of living together, it was all on his terms.

The car park had been full that night so we had each had to park elsewhere, but he was closer and would take me to mine. We walked in silence to his car, and when I got in beside him he patted my hand and said it would be alright, and I knew it would not. Sadness engulfed me, and this time I was the one to flinch.

Chapter Eight

Spring was coming and I was undergoing an unintended change. My lack of appetite had achieved something I had wrestled with for years, I had become thin without even trying. I also had a solicitor who told me to "keep up my spending", for which I had little heart, but I needed to buy some new clothes.

I took no joy in this, as I might have done in the past; I don't think I took joy in anything, it was just a matter of getting by. Nick and I had stopped seeing one another, not least because I had begun to hate him.

'I may have betrayed you in love, but I won't when it comes to money,' he had said, but he had.

In the months leading up to the moment of truth, those bits of paper he had so frequently asked me to sign had been all about shifting money into an account he had in Jersey. Mrs Clark had been an aberration, I wanted a divorce.

I was now living in Laura's house, had succeeded in extracting the nice cat, and had taken a lodger, a policeman whose own marriage had just split up and who was in a similar state of mind. But he was rarely there, and alone I would suddenly fall victim to howling, which I hated. Julie included me in social events and the people I met were enthralled by my story, which I couldn't stop telling. But something in me was beginning to feel ready to move on. 'You need to find a new man,' someone had said to me.

I had never thought of Adam as being that man,

we'd both known it had been a one-off and were now back in our uncomplicated admiration for each other with just that extra edge. Somebody suggested computer dating, but I had already thought of it, I was now raring to go.

My mindset was "nothing to lose" and I was probably embarking on this new adventure too soon, but I've always been impatient. Besides, I was no longer young, even a bit old, although I didn't feel it.

One of the photographers at work took my picture and then helped me to load it onto the dating site. I went through the list of questions, the answers to which would attract or repel. I was honest about being a smoker but discovered later that most people lied about this, and much else. My profile had me as tall, slim and blonde, which was all true, but somehow not in my head, where I remained big, fat and not really blonde.

The first man I met was a retired bookie from Southend, although he had put Romford, explaining that this was so that he could get a good fifty mile radius, something not possible if you lived on the coast. This was a lie that I liked because it indicated a bit of cleverness.

He was of medium height, slight build, balding and with a pronounced Essex accent. We met in a pub halfway between our two locations and told one another our stories, even though this was not advised on the dating site – don't talk about past loves. He was a widower but did not seem too sad, just lonely. When I told him my story, he said my husband should be shot. When we parted we kissed one another on each cheek, then he held out his arms and said 'One in the middle'. We said we would meet again. I had decided not to make comparisons, and I dare say he felt the same.

Before our next meeting I lost it completely at work, the awful uncontrollable howling. I had been out all day at an event I had to cover for the paper and when I got back to the office, the howling overcame me while I was still outside. I went round to the side of the building to hide but someone came by and heard me. Later I found myself in the editor's office, the howling unabated, but I was beyond embarrassment. That night I was supposed to be seeing Southend again, but instead, I ended up in London.

I'd let it all come out in the editor's office, all that had happened, the stinging things said, recounted through the awful howling. The editor, half my age, recognised extremis, telling me he couldn't believe how I had carried on working and how I was well out of it as far as the marriage was concerned. The trouble was, I still didn't think so.

I can't remember how it happened, but I must have given my old friend's number to the colleague who had found me outside. I also gave her Southend's number and she called him too, and told me that he sounded like a lovely man. My old friend, who had been about to set out for the opera, dropped everything and came to fetch me. She had phoned Nick when it had first happened and he had told her it was sad but he would make sure I was financially okay. She told me now that she wasn't going to say anything against him in case we got back together. She told me too that of all her friends' husbands, she had liked him better than most, even though she had not thought much of him to begin with. 'He drops his "g's",' she'd noticed. Her husband, a lot older, had died in his eighties. We agreed that hers was the better situation because she still had the love.

After a few days she drove me back to Cambridge and the next phase of my life as a slim, free person. Southend came to spend the night and we sat on my sofa holding hands like teenagers at the cinema. When we went upstairs he had his clothes off in a trice, but things weren't working. 'He's nervous, like his owner,' he said. We were kind to one another but we didn't meet again.

When I got home after work I would trawl through the faces and profiles, feeling vaguely uneasy, even reluctant; but it had become addictive, the most basic human quest. I didn't want to be alone.

Most of the men profiled on the site were no-hopers, but I expect many of them thought the same about me. Although a journalist, I had found it incredibly challenging to write about myself. My interests sounded frumpy, "knitting", "crossword puzzles". What sort of music did I like? Whatever was on Classic FM when Radio 4 had the occasional duff programme. What kind of TV? I had given up on that, couldn't concentrate, and the dramas seemed tepid beside my own.

I read profiles of men who claimed to like cooking

and 'having a night in', others who spent all their spare time mountain biking and having 'a good sense of humour'. They liked golf and football and tinkering with cars and writing poetry. They liked themselves.

Most had posted appallingly bad photos of themselves, some you could barely see, although perhaps this was deliberate. I quickly became uncharitable towards these poor lonely fellows. Then I found one with no picture at all, just that outline of a person they put in the photo box when nothing has been supplied. But the man with no face was in Cambridge, so I read what he had to say. It was eloquent and honest, he wanted a long-term passionate relationship with someone who 'understood the needs of a carer'. He said he was an academic. I sent him a brief message asking to know more. He responded by asking if he could call me, saying his subscription to the site was about to expire. I sent him my number. Okay, I shouldn't have done, but caution no longer interested me.

I heard nothing and in the meantime began a friendship with a man I had met through work and with whom I occasionally had lunch when he wanted me to write something about his latest business venture. I had never found him the least bit attractive, he was short and fat and myopic. He had bad skin and had recently parted from his wife, who was a pretty woman with an empty head. I had met her once or twice, they had come to a party at my house, and she had been among a group of us at a corporate event at the races. They had seemed ill-matched, I couldn't understand why she might ever have fancied him, but there had been something there, gone sour. I remembered how at the races there had been cream teas served in the hospitality box and she had piled a load of scones onto his plate and smothered them in strawberry jam and cream and gone on and on at him to eat the lot, goading his greed. However, he had resisted, her manner, no doubt, spoiling his appetite. She had become increasingly drunk and obstreperous and he the former, but lapsing into what seemed like a careless acceptance of his lot. I think that was one of the occasions when I felt thankful for my own marriage.

During the lunch, our stories came out, and when we parted, I agreed to meet again, for dinner. This time we both knew that the markers had shifted, although I had no intention of going beyond a friendship. The evening went well, as had the several lunches we'd had over the years, he had plenty to say and it was interesting. He also listened to what I said, something Nick had not done for years, for how long had he found me boring?

When he took me home, I invited him in for coffee, and the conversation continued, somehow straying into a past life when he had been a folk singer. A folk singer! Gloomy, gloomy, strum, strum, woe is me and the whole wide world.

'Go on, then.'

And he did, striding straight into an immediately captivating song which he sang in perfect pitch, remembering all the words as if he'd been up practising all night. I wanted more. For the first time in months, I was taken over by something else.

We sat up late into the night and he kept on singing. The words were nonsense, but his voice was intoxicating. I made a bed up for him on the sofa and in the morning he was gone, leaving a note saying he'd had the best night in years. I saw him again, of course I did, I wanted to hear him sing some more, find that small patch of reprieve. The next time we met I was to stay the night at his place, simply so that I could drink more than two glasses of wine. He had a flat above a shop, a place he had rented after leaving the marital home. It was old, Victorian, perhaps earlier, with high ceilings and intriguing passageways. He had an ancient four-poster bed with heavy velvet drapes, and a huge television positioned so that you could sit up in a nest of pillows and watch.

The bed, too big for any of the rooms which might have been designated for sleeping, was in the corner of a large living room in which there were also several armchairs with ornate gilded arms. I sat in one after we'd come back from the restaurant, and waited to see what might happen next. I didn't really care what that might be.

We settled down with more wine, and he switched on a music video on his big telly and the first song was that plaintive one where someone who has lost their lover to another still has hopes 'Let it be me'.

In my entire life, I had never before been affected by song lyrics. He spotted it almost before I did, because he was watching me closely, like the ever so patient night angler waiting on the edge of the river for his catch.

'Shall I put something else on,' he said, looking concerned. I shook my head. 'Let it be me' and not her. 'Let it be me'.

I am sitting here in this man's flat, somewhere I never thought I would be, where I should not be because my real home is elsewhere. I apologise. To him? To myself? I've no idea. The song ends.

Chapter Nine

I was at work when the telephone call came. His name was Amit and he had a lovely educated Indian voice. I suppose I have an educated English voice. After we had exchanged a few words, he said, 'There is chemistry here,' at just the right speed.

I didn't ask why it had taken him so long to call, what would be the point? Perhaps he had been trying out other women, but I had not been idle. I had slept in the four-poster bed and discovered that a physically unattractive man can be a brilliant kisser. I had decided to like him and he had decided to go to his doctor and see if anything could be done about his poor old willy, which, like Southend's, would not do what he wanted it to do. He had very white legs and a tattoo on one thigh, nothing like "I love mum", it looked like a Chinese symbol, I didn't ask. He kept his vest on. But I had decided to like him.

He took me to nice restaurants and the conversation never stopped, but we were still talking about business, more so than before we had taken to the four-poster bed, when we were both in marriages that, certainly for my part, had seemed unassailable. He wanted us to go into business together, whatever he was saying seemed to lead again and again to this idea.

One night he said something which was not a good idea. Someone he knew had seen us at one of the restaurants. He laughed and told me word had got around that he was there with 'some old bird', the emphasis on 'old'. He was not unintelligent, far from it, but why say such a thing? I didn't really care, I was still too numb from the big upset, although maybe I didn't know it; and there were the pills, piles of them I was taking.

Even so, I became like a teenager waiting for his calls, wanting to be wanted, still terrified of being alone.

Amit had told me that he was going to be away and would not be in touch for a while, and I suppose I had sort of dismissed him from the playlist, for all his 'chemistry'. But I wondered what he looked like, no photograph having been with his profile on the dating site. Then he called me from Cape Town. He said he was at a conference and this led on to some questions from me and he said he was a professor at Cambridge and told me the name of the college. A little bit of internet searching and I found him, oh dear.

But I was not looking for 'looks'. I had fallen for the way Nick looked, tall, well-built, but not fat, and an arresting presence, even if he did drop his 'g's. I peered and peered at the picture of Amit, the expressionless face, but that was to be expected on college websites, no one smiling.

Then he was back, and wanted us to meet, and the voice was enough for me to agree. It was one of those cavernous bar restaurants you get in every city, faux-rustic, old tennis rackets and curios from junk shops pinned to the walls, paintwork deliberately distressed. I arrived first and found a table some way from the entrance, perhaps I didn't want him to see me from outside and decide not to come in, although I don't remember thinking that at the time, but I was still more bruised and battered than I fully realised. What I was doing was like stepping out into traffic without looking, just hoping for the best and trusting to whatever it was in which I should no longer have any faith at all.

And suddenly he was there, standing beside me, and I would not have recognised him if he had not me. He must have lost much weight since the college picture, he was medium height, a good figure in an expensive grey suit, a full head of slightly greying hair, and a face I knew I was going to kiss.

He was married, but I'd guessed that. He was a carer to his wife. The family home was in the north, where he had held a previous professorial chair before retiring and taking up a part-time post in Cambridge. I don't know whether I ever entirely believed the 'carer' bit, it was more likely that he wanted sex while he was in Cambridge, which was far enough away from home to be safe. None of this mattered. The 'chemistry' was undeniable, I could feel it in my groin.

It's not easy to remember the things you say on first meeting someone you fancy, the pheromones must take over, even when it is far too late in life for them to serve any useful purpose.

The talking continued until suddenly he said that he wanted to make love to me, and without hesitating, I said 'yes', that was all. We stood up and he kissed me on the mouth, which slightly took me aback.

'Don't be coy,' he said.

'I'm not coy.'

We semi marched to his college rooms, which were no more than five minutes away. We passed someone he knew, and I wondered whether they knew, whether I was one of many to have made this march. I didn't care. I was free to do as I liked. I didn't care.

There were several flights of old wooden stairs to climb before we reached his door, and on the way up my phone rang. I glanced at the screen and turned it off.

'Don't be unkind,' he said, gently. The call had been from the folk-singer, whose calls so short a time ago I had yearned to receive.

This was the first time I had visited the rooms of a college professor, there was a living area with a big white sofa, a small dining table and chairs, his desk and computer. Beyond, I could see the bedroom, white linen, a double bed.

We turned to one another and so it began. After a while we got up from the bed and sat by the window, both of us naked, but there was hardly any light in the room. I gazed out across the Cambridge roof scape and felt the dampness trickle from me. I looked down at myself and for the first time realised that I had become slim, that my legs were good when I had never thought they could be anything but bad, that my stomach was flat. He had lovely legs, I always liked his legs. He had a bit of a stomach, but not too much, and his skin was so smooth.

He was saying the sort of things a man says to a woman with whom he has no intention of having much more than sex, and I was going along with it, lost in the notion of being the other woman as opposed to the wife. I didn't consider her for a moment, any more than I had Nick's wife when we had started our affair, or, presumably had the woman he now described as his partner. I had rude names for her, had been unable to stop myself from saying them. Nick had said he didn't mind what I said about him as long as I didn't say anything against his 'new partner'. How that hurt, his 'new partner'. And how unreasonable that I should be forbidden to insult her.

I didn't ask what was wrong with Amit's wife, I didn't want to know, didn't want to make it my business, and suspected that even if he told me, I would not believe him. It was a wonderfully clear night, the sky full of stars, and I was heady with what had just happened, with the promised chemistry, which was undoubtedly there.

'The important thing is never to be unkind,' he was saying, stroking my leg. He had written in his profile that he was looking for a long-standing passionate relationship, and I thought I had found it. I thought I would not mind an intermittent, semi-secret relationship, that it might suit me very well.

I stood up and reached for some of my clothes, but he halted me, 'Did you think I was going to make love to you only once?' It was not really a question.

'I love your ivory skin,' he said later, running his hand over my body. 'Do you like my black cock?' Of course I did.

Chapter Ten

I wasn't quite sure how I felt when I discovered that it had been offered to a friend. Since moving to Cambridge I had got to know a woman who lived in the same road. She was a year or so younger than me, on her own, two marriages behind her, we had things in common, and I liked her. We had quickly developed an intimacy in conversation that would more normally have taken years. She too was internet dating, but had been at it a lot longer than me; she too had spotted the Amit profile and been similarly intrigued. She had twice had dinner with him and the second time had gone back to his rooms, where he had assumed the same scenario which had led me to his bed. But she had baulked at it, and he had told her 'You win some, you lose some'.

If this knowledge fazed me a little, I didn't let it stop me from seeing him again, and again. I was not only entranced by him physically, I was also falling for his mind. He talked to me about history and economics and explained the story behind the division between Sunni and Shia. He told me about his childhood in India, his Hindu upbringing in an upper class family of academics and poets, political trouble he had got himself into when he was barely out of his teens, torture, terror, escape. There was an edge of doubt in me, but I chose not to indulge it.

It had been some months now since I had seen Nick, but I needed to go the house to sort out some of my stuff, a visit I was dreading. I thought I had managed to get myself onto a sort of even keel but I knew I was still fragile and didn't know how I would feel going back to the house, the home I had made, all the associations.

It was a beautiful day, half an hour driving through the sunshine, turning through the gates, seeing the lovely old house, waiting for a moment or two in the car to see how I felt. It didn't seem real, that this was no longer my home, all those times, countless, I had driven back here from work, from shopping, coming home from holidays, leaving the car without a pause, running up the stone steps to the front door, up the next flight to the internal front door and every night turning to go into the study where Nick would still be at his desk, kissing him, asking about his day, then heading off for the kitchen to prepare supper, a pattern that had been forever.

This time I knocked at the door, like a stranger. Nick took a while to appear, I didn't think it then, but he was probably hiding any paperwork he didn't want me to see; I discovered later that he had become paranoid about me snooping, something I had never done.

Having let me in he immediately returned to the study, his body language making it clear he had things to get on with. We were both polite, superficial greetings, we might as well have shaken hands, although that would have been too much, we were not touching, that had become out of bounds.

I went upstairs to find the bits and pieces I needed

and without thinking went to the bedroom to take something from my bedside cupboard. As I bent down I glanced across the bed and on my grandmother's old washstand on Nick's side was a photograph. It was her. She was sitting very upright, very posed, in a green dress, her hands in her lap. Her face, unsmiling, was plain, an overlong, flat nose, nothing to be seen in the eyes. Nothing, of course, to indicate the wonderful body which looked thirty years younger than it was. How such things stuck in the mind.

It didn't cross my mind that my own body had reverted to an unexpected youthfulness, in my head I was still the overweight woman who was too old to fancy, even in the face of evidence to the contrary.

Suddenly I felt I no longer had any right to be in this room. I looked down at my side of the bed and imagined her in it. Quickly, I found what I could that I wanted, which wasn't much but might have been more if I could have stayed there any longer.

I collected one or two more things and then went back downstairs. I knocked on the study door and pushed it open. Nick had stood up and was coming towards me as if he didn't want me to come in. Then he said, 'Would you like some lunch?' And he seemed to want to do this. 'We'll go down to The Feathers.'

This was the pub in the town square where every Friday in recent memory I had gone to meet him after the early evening drink at the pub in Cambridge where I went with Tony. Nick would be there with some of the people who worked for us, people I had liked but before long wouldn't. And, of course, the last time I had gone there was when Nick had treated me with such indifference, when all the signs had been there and yet I had ignored them, been unaware of the slightest threat.

We left the house, crossed the huge driveway, which was more like a car park, through the gates and started down the hill into town. There was a loud meow behind us and the yowling cat was scurrying to catch up.

'He's never done that before,' Nick said.

We chased him back to the house and set off again, walking airily apart, I wasn't sure why I was doing this, agreeing to the lunch. We took a table outside and almost straightaway he was talking about the situation with his new partner, that still she would not leave her husband. A spike of venom ran through me as I remembered how, the night it had all come out, she had told him she did not want her husband to find out, but that she wanted to 'carry on dating', never mind the wreckage.

And then I was telling him that I was in a similar situation, that I was seeing an Indian professor who was married and could not leave his wife. I made it sound as if he might have wanted to, although I knew this was not the case. Nick didn't seem to be that interested. Our food came, but I could do no more than play with it. I was saying something when Nick made an observation which had nothing to do with what I had been talking about, and I remembered how he had done this in the past, because he must have found me boring; but this time I didn't let it pass.

'There you go again,' I said, and he knew what I meant.

He was looking at me now.

'You've completely reinvented yourself,' he said, as if informing me of a revelation that had just come to him.

Some people we vaguely knew came by and waved to us. I wondered whether they had heard what had happened, whether they thought we were back together.

I went to the loo and when I came out Nick had gone. I looked up the road and saw him walking quickly towards home.

Later that day he sent me a text: 'You've done really well.' Then he repeated what he had said about my reinvention. How dare he!

Chapter Eleven

The end of the university term had come and Amit had returned to his home in the north, I would not see him for at least two months. I allowed myself to feel romantic about him, to think about him and enjoy the thoughts, but I had put up a barrier to keep me from further harm. The howling had more or less abated. I had been seeing the counsellor suggested by my doctor, and realised that the only time I did break down now was when I went to see her. This is not to say there was anything wrong with her, she was a quiet, kind, bland person, whose job it was to listen, which she did very well.

I had started seeing her not long after leaving Nick. The first couple of times I had already been in a state before getting there. Calmly she would hand me the box of tissues. Her consulting room was in a rundown building on the edge of Cambridge, the furnishings redolent of the sort of 1940s sitting room you saw in the old black and white films like Brief Encounter; if you were not already feeling gloomy, the room would do it for you.

The first time I went I had talked a lot about Nick, and towards the end of the allotted time she had suddenly declared that she would love to meet him, that he sounded like a classic, one hundred percent narcissist. This had taken me aback, as it had never occurred to me, even though I now saw that it was patently true. I realised that her hypothetical wish to meet him was entirely academic.

I told her about how I had suggested he and I go to Relate, how he had said he didn't mind, but hadn't realised they saw couples where one party had no intention of giving up the third. All this stuff amounted to renewed stabbings, more tissues. I don't know what I expected to gain from these sessions as they didn't seem to make me feel any better.

Another awful howling episode had been when I had gone to see Nick's brother and his wife, stupidly assuming they would be there for me. They didn't want to know. I didn't go there again. They too had found displacement activities, perhaps it ran in the family, anything to avoid engaging with me. Long ago, on a bleak night, they had turned up on our doorstep, it was very late. It was the first time I met her, just a girl then, twenty years his junior, she had been lodging with the family. His wife had thrown them out. They had stayed with us until they found a place to rent. Blood is thicker than.

The girl had turned into a madam, or perhaps she had always been so. The wife had been vilified, constantly, because she was the wife. She didn't deserve it, they both knew that, but her lack of culpability could be endured only by finding fault. What it seemed to amount to was a lack of enthusiasm for adventurous sex.

This theme had returned. The first thing madam had asked me was whether I had done all I should in the bedroom. Little things stick in the mind, I had once been in their bedroom and seen a very large carrot on the bedside table.

I answered her question with gusto, threw in sodomy. I really didn't care what I said. I think they did. I think they had seen me out of curiosity and now that was satisfied I could get on my way. The last time I saw them, when there had been the displacement activities, it had finally dawned on me that I was not welcome. Madam had come out with me to the car and put on kindness, perhaps it was genuine. 'You'll get through this,' she had said, stroking my arm. At the time it didn't feel possible.

My summer of madness continued, my adventures via the dating site. One evening I opened the site, ready to trawl through profiles of men who had a good sense of humour even if their photos rebuffed this. They seemed as sad as me and probably were, even if astride motor bikes or hazily pictured on yachts, more often looking as if they had just come out of prison, staring straight at the camera, grim-faced, hoping against the odds for a last chance. It was a sorry business, this search among faces no longer attractive, profiles that spelt desperation. I didn't think I was there yet, although they probably did.

But tonight there was a message from someone who had seen my picture and wanted to know more. In his picture he was wearing a panama hat and he was smiling. He was a retired drama teacher, he said, lived in south London. I responded to him and almost immediately he came back to me, how seeing my picture had brightened his day, it didn't take much to flatter me then, grasp at anything.

He came up to Cambridge one Saturday night, we had agreed to meet in a pub on the river. I walked along the towpath, the evening sunshine warm and bathing the river and trees with amber highlights. I felt quite jaunty, wearing a short, multi-coloured, figure-hugging dress, a million miles from the long black shirts and blouses in which I had shrouded my fat self for years.

I spotted him as soon as I rounded the huge weeping willow tree beside the pub, the same pub where I had met Amit one night earlier in the year when it was cold and grey and he was sitting there alone outside because the place was closed. This new man, Rod, spotted me at the same moment. He stood up and I could see in his face that I had passed the first test, and because I had, it didn't matter that much that he might have failed mine. We had a drink, talked, I could never remember those first conversations unless something outlandish was said, and it rarely was, because you didn't go to all the trouble of travelling from south London or Southend to fall at the first fence. You wanted to give it your best shot, even if you knew it was all just a waste of time.

Rod suggested we go to the cinema so we set off across Midsummer Common, arm in arm, the heartbroken on a mission. I can't remember the film, only that we started snogging like teenagers from a very long time ago, when we had been teenagers. I didn't mind. None of it mattered. See what happens.

On the way home there were more kisses amid the darkness of the trees. He was divorced, three children.

He was adrift, like me. We both wanted the other to be worth a bit of effort, although I had no intention of giving up Amit, who I would not see again until the university term began in the autumn. A summer fling, I thought.

He didn't stay that night, he had a friend nearby, a man he had not seen in years, barely an acquaintance but who had agreed to let him have a bed for the night in view of his endeavour with me. The following weekend he came again, arriving on Saturday morning with a bottle of wine which I put in the fridge. We went out for a walk along the river and when we returned he put his hat on the table and we went upstairs with a tacit understanding. Despite what Amit had said, I'd never been coy and was undressed and in bed before Rod. We had drawn the curtains but they were white and the light came through. I watched him removing his clothes until something which looked rather like an old-fashioned lavatory chain was revealed around his waist. This was an unexpected accessory for a man who wore a panama hat, and it didn't end like a belt but was looped under his genitals.

Years ago such an accoutrement would have turned me off, even alarmed me, but I was lacking self-preservation, completely in the zone of what-does-it-matter, it even crossed my mind that he might hurt me, physically, and I really didn't care. I even laughed at the chain, although I knew mockery was inadvisable in such circumstances; but he laughed too, and that made the whole thing more or less okay.

I heard my policeman lodger come home, and

perhaps that was a comfort. The retired drama teacher and I flailed about in bed for a while, but nothing much happened, perhaps I should not have laughed at the chain. He said he had to get back to Croydon that night and while he was putting on his jacket I handed him the bag he had put on the table and felt the coldness of the bottle of wine. We exchanged glances.

After he had gone, I sat down and wondered whether I could go on seeing a man who had furtively retrieved the gift he had brought. The lodger had spotted the hat.

The following weekend I met another man, one of two Jameses, in this saga. We had arranged to meet at a garden centre with a café. I could see straightaway he had lied about his age, but I wasn't going to dismiss him out of hand. We sat down for coffee and he told me about his wife's long illness and recent death, the tediousness of having to take her to hospital all the time. He was weary and worn out but with a spark of hope for the last lap.

When he got round to asking about me, I gave him a brief resume. Then he wanted to know if I was seeing anyone else, and as I have always had a tendency to be uncontrollably truthful, I said yes, three, which it was at the time, with another James coming on the scene.

He wanted to know if I was sleeping with them and I nodded, yes, two. He giggled, he was being turned on by this. He said I was an extremely attractive woman and he wanted to see me again. I bet he did. I smiled at him across the table and thought how repulsive I would find his moley old skin. I thought of Amit,

smooth, unblemished. I wanted Amit with an exquisite
ache I would nurture for the rest of the summer.

Chapter Twelve

There were still moments when I felt as if I was not living my real life, that it was all waiting for me to return, one day I would simply drive back to the old house, go inside without knocking and there would be Nick, in the study, behind his desk. Without thinking, I would go over and kiss him, and he would kiss me back before continuing with whatever work he was doing.

'Nice day?'

'Yes. And yours?' No waiting for answers.

I would go through the hallway to the kitchen and start to prepare supper. I would pour two glasses of wine, take one to him. We would smile at one another. I would listen to The Archers while I cooked the meal and then Front Row. I would look out at the tremendous view from the kitchen window, across the flatlands towards Cambridge, take it in and think how much I liked it and how I would have it forever.

With the food cooking, I would take my glass to the drawing room, settle on one of the sofas and switch on the telly. It would be some early evening easy viewing, for a time it had been EastEnders until I couldn't stand all the trauma. I would go through my post, find something in it that would amuse Nick, take it to show him, to share it.

When I had first taken my job I had been half-hearted about the prospect, I had been trying for a long time to make it as a writer, but although I had succeeded in finding an agent and a publisher and had written half a dozen or more books which had been seriously reviewed, I was not going to reach that plateau of acceptable sales. I had been dumped by both publisher and agent and although I had managed to get a couple more books published, it was never going to be more than, well, a hobby, although I hated that word, it sounded too trivial to attach to my continuing compulsion to write.

The public relations agency I had set up to allow me time to write my own stuff and with the encouragement of Nick, who had seen the bad times coming for his own business, was running its course. I had never liked the work, but it had saved the day for us. Now that another business had taken off for Nick, we no longer needed to pander to the egotistical clients and their love of superfluous adjectives in anything we wrote about them. So, I should go back to my first love, newspapers, and, miraculously, I had found a job. But I had been self-employed for such a long time and I knew I was going to feel like an unbroken horse going back into a regular job. Hence the mixed feelings, plus a heavy sense of failure, the unlikelihood of any further books with my name on the spine.

The weekend before I was due to start my new job we'd been invited to a lunch party with a friend who was also a writer, and her husband who did something mysterious in the Foreign Office. There were three other couples there, a man who had won a television talent contest many years before and who now made promotional videos, his guitar long gone. His wife was an artist who we didn't think was very good. In the other two couples there was a specialist publisher, a furniture restorer, and a man who had briefly enjoyed a high flying career, and his wife who had had to put up with him when it had crashed.

We had met all these people before, knew their back stories. They were all high octane, I tended to feel lesser when we were with them, yet I wanted us to be part of this set, where the conversation never ran out and I took each of them at face value, even if Nick didn't.

On this particular occasion, jovial to the edge of excess, they all wanted to know about my new job, even though I had yet to start it, so there was very little I could tell them, and my own mood was subdued. On the Monday my life was going to change and I wasn't sure about any of it, going back to your first love can be a mistake.

That evening, back home, I was still quiet. Nick came and sat beside me in the drawing room. 'You know, all those people today would give a lot to get the job you've got.' He paused. 'And none of them would have stood a chance.'

Chapter Thirteen

Only days after I had found out about Nick's affair I went to see a solicitor. It seemed the obvious and necessary thing to do. She was a thin, sharp woman with a hard face and a clever smile. I don't remember a lot of what was said, it was difficult to concentrate. We sat either side of a table in a bare room. She told me it was vital that I maintain my spending, a necessity which had to be explained to me. It was about being able to demonstrate to a judge the amount of money I needed to continue living in the manner to which I had become accustomed. It stank. I didn't think I was like that. I thought of a friend who had gone out and bought two expensive rings the day after discovering that her marriage was over. I could not imagine having the heart for such shopping, any shopping, I'd lost my mojo in that department, a state of affairs that continued for months.

I did ask the solicitor how much the divorce was likely to cost. She asked how much I had. I told her. It was about a hundred thousand, money left from my father's estate, the last bit, with which I had been about to buy a flat to let. If I'd gone ahead with that I would have been skint. The solicitor laughed and assured me she and her colleagues would be able to spend what I had.

Uneasy? When you go to a solicitor, when it's too soon, you lean on them too much. You call them late at night with a worry that is just too urgent to leave until the morning. You rely on them because they are unequivocally on your side and there can be no one else who knows any better than they do what you should do and what you should not.

When the first bill came I was frightened. Nothing had been achieved, nothing really done, as far as I could tell, and yet here was this massive bill. I didn't know who to turn to, so I sent it to Nick and asked him what I should do.

Nick hated solicitors, he thought they were people who profited from the misery of others, he despised them but it was also in his nature to enjoy a spat with them; he always thought he could win, and even when he didn't, which had been more often the case, he could convince himself that in some way he had.

He paid the bill, warned me against the venality of lawyers. He paid the next bill too. I could see it only as guilt.

I've mentioned before my propensity to tell the truth, and in me it is a fault. I wanted everyone to know how guilty Nick was, and in the process of telling them diminished myself.

One night soon after I'd left him, I went to the theatre in Cambridge, tickets I already had, took Julie. In the interval I saw a couple I knew. She was a woman who did church flowers and he was a self-satisfied stuffed shirt. They came over to me and she enquired after the family.

'Oh, they're fine, but Nick's taken up with a prostitute he met on a sex site, so I've left him.' Julie, known for her own delight in saying the outrageous, quailed beside me. 'Oh, Lottie,' she said. The couple had already moved away.

I told everyone I met. I couldn't stop myself. Julie had a party at her house and my story took it over. It was months before I realised I had to stop, and even then it would sometimes slip out, like pandering to an addiction to shock value.

Why did I do it? Why would I want anyone to know that my husband had gone off me and sought sex elsewhere, desperate enough to go online in a dangerous zone. In time, I wished I had kept quiet, because I knew that this would now be forever how people thought of me. Sexual matters are like that. Think of anyone well known, of whom you have no real knowledge, but if they have been involved in any sort of sexual scandal that is what you think of first.

With some of the people I told, I would add to what Nick had done that there had been no need, compounding the vulgarity.

Soon after it all happened I went to see my brother. He lived in the north, not that far and a journey I had done many times in the car, but I felt incapable of driving such a distance so went by train. It was a complicated route, two or three changes, up to an hour spent on cold and windy platforms where smoking was not allowed. I stared at the tracks and thought of people who threw themselves under trains. I tried to keep thinking of the night I had spent with Adam, the only good thing to hold on to, my fall-back reverie.

My brother met me at the final station, a bleak place where every surface seemed covered with ice. I had called him the day after Nick's confession, said he had no need to alter his holiday dates now. I had planned to have a dinner for Nick's birthday, hiring a room in one of the Cambridge colleges. It was going to be a big birthday and I had wanted to make it memorable. I had already paid the considerable deposit and drawn up the guest list. When I told Nick about this, this surprise event which would no longer happen, he had said he would have hated it because he would have been expected to make a speech. I hadn't thought of that. But I had never thought he hated making speeches. He had made some particularly good ones. They were considered and often poignant, and would surprise and delight me with their perspicacity.

My brother had the same sort of insight, although in every other way he was so very not like Nick. That night we sat round an open fire in the remote cottage where Charles and Mary lived. The rooms were already decked with Christmas decorations and the smell of pine cones was brought out by the fire.

I talked and talked, going over the same old ground, mesmerized by the fire as the words poured out, victimising myself: it was my fault for putting on weight, that was it.

Mary sighed and said, 'No, it would have happened anyway.' And in such moments you know that others have always seen what you have been too close to, too wrapped up in the coupledom to spot.

My thinking was wild. When Charles said I should change my will as soon as possible, I thought he might be suggesting that Nick might try to do away with me.

In truth he possibly thought I might try to do away with myself. Charles was very much a family man and would be thinking of my daughters and what they might be denied if something happened. But I was not thinking of killing myself, I couldn't do that to my children, and I was not, strangely, depressed, just hugely sad. I knew what depression was, it obliterated hope, and that I had not lost.

Even so, I felt careless in the sense that I took less care, nothing in the day-to-day business of life seemed to matter all that much, and perhaps this was what Charles could see.

The weekend in the north gave me comfort, not just being with Charles and Mary, it was something to do with the distance, which doesn't make any sense. It might simply have been a physical representation of what I most wanted to do, escape what had to be dealt with, albeit briefly. 'I need to get away' people say.

Charles and Mary, who didn't seem to need to get away from anything, had a house in Spain where they spent a good deal of time and where they would be going immediately after Christmas. I too had a house abroad, a stone cottage I had bought in France with money left to me by my father.

Nick and I had been spending summer holidays in the Charente for some years, renting gites. We would go to nearby towns and look in the windows of estate agents, peering at pictures of what sometimes looked like no more than a pile of stones with a wonky window. We had met Brits who had bought such ruins and devoted themselves to restoration projects that would take years.

The houses the French seemed to favour were new and looked like cow sheds, built with the proceeds from the sale of the ruins to fanciful foreigners. Poof! We were all mad.

I took a week off work and Nick and I flew to Bergerac, hired a car and set off in earnest to find a French property. It was December so nothing looked its best. We stayed in a small hotel overlooking one of those long 'squares' they have in the larger French villages. Two rows of trees ran its length, winter-abandoned chairs and tables were stacked along the middle, all seemed quiet and closed. I loved it, this out-of-season reality.

And not everything was shut, the estate agents would open if you rang a number. That week we saw twenty or more houses, I liked some, Nick liked some, but they were not the same ones. A question we asked was why they were being sold, and on more than one property were told that the couple selling had parted. They were Brits who had come to live here only to discover that they didn't really like one another when it came to all day together without the hinterland of friends. We looked at one another smugly. Not us.

On the last day we found the stone cottage, high above the medieval village where we were staying. This was perfect, as the week we had spent at the hotel had proved to be an additional enticement, we had become acquainted with some of the ex-pats who scratched a living looking after other ex-pat homes. They told us their stories and perhaps we thought that these were people with whom we could carouse when we spent our holidays here and, in time, more than that, perhaps we would come for a month or two at a time.

We spent three holidays in the stone cottage before we decided to sell. When we saw the working expats again, they didn't recognise us, and the Brits we overheard in the hotel bar were of the Hermes-scarf-wearing variety with husbands determinedly old-bufferish.

Subsequently I realised that this sojourn was over for Nick before it came to an end for me. The last time we went, he was absent even when he was there.

Chapter Fourteen

Simone

Nick was with his wife in France. I didn't give her a lot of thinking, that was the only way. Since February, when I first met him, I had used up my holiday, a day at a time, so I could see him. The company I worked for didn't care. It had a pool of cleaners and we covered for each other.

He had talked to me about going to France, how he couldn't not go. I understood this, but pretended I didn't. Our last meeting before he went away I was cool with him. And it wasn't just because he was going away. It was the hotel. It was a dirty place we'd been before. Why had he booked it again? I wasn't worth any better. That's how I felt.

'I don't like this place,' was the first thing I said to him. 'It's cheap.'

I looked straight at him when I said this and I could see him thinking 'she's not paying'. But at the same time I could see he knew he had made a mistake and was worried he wouldn't have such a good time with me.

'I'll make contact every day,' he said, assuming that's what I wanted from him. 'It's only two weeks, barely that.'

But two weeks can seem an awfully long time, especially when your man is away with his wife; and he was mine, I knew that.

I didn't think about anything like this when I first met Nick; all I wanted was a bit of life, a bit of it just for myself. The women I worked with talked a lot about online dating, it seemed to be like a hobby for them. Some had been doing it for years, would say they had given it up, but always started again, like smoking or drinking. I didn't do any of these things. I didn't want to. I never had. It was bad enough being a passive smoker at home, being passive in everything.

The other thing about online dating was I didn't understand how the women I worked with got away with it. Some were married or living with a man. And surely it was dangerous, not just the possibility of being found out, but the men they met, they didn't know anything about them.

I said this once, to one of the women. We were mopping the floor in the school hall, working our way from either end to meet in the middle. She'd been talking the whole time, shouting really because the hall was so big, shouting about a new man she had met, what a great night she'd had and all the money he'd spent on her.

'All the men I've met, there's never been a problem,' she said. 'But maybe I've just been lucky.'

She was the one who told me about Illicit Encounters. I didn't know there were websites like that. I did Facebook a lot with my daughter when she was home. I knew how to work the web, but I had always been open about it, never secretive, there was no need. I had to think of a way to be private if I started looking at pictures of men who wanted sex.

Elizabeth would not forgive me if she found out, she loved Derek.

But there were no pictures, of course there couldn't be, it was illicit. The best thing was that women did not have to pay anything to join, the men had to, but not the women. All you had to do was post a description of yourself and see what happened. I could have done with Elizabeth's help writing about myself, but of course I couldn't ask her.

I had a few tries, but there was nothing I wanted to say about myself, nothing I thought would do me any good, so it ended up *Simone, 38, Asian. Cambridgeshire*, which said too little and too much.

It got dangerous right from the start. I had a huge number of men trying to meet me. The first night my laptop kept pinging and Derek noticed pretty quickly.

'You're very popular tonight,' he said, rolling yet another cigarette.

'I think there's something wrong with it.' I couldn't think what else to say.

'Give Betty a call, she'll know how to put it right.' I didn't like his name for Elizabeth. Nobody would call the Queen that.

'She's much too busy with her studies. And please don't call her that.'

I took the machine upstairs and turned off the sound before looking at all this traffic. Some of it was frightening. The things they wanted to do with me. But I kept on looking until I heard Derek calling me.

I stuffed the laptop at the back of my wardrobe and went back downstairs to the fug of the sitting room.

I hate smoking, having to breathe in what's come from someone else's nose. Derek looked like a dragon the way he puffed out the smoke from his nostrils. He spent most of the day just sitting there doing all the things that were bad for him. He drank whisky, which was the most disgusting thing I had ever tasted. Tasting him disgusted me too. He smelled like mouse.

'You alright, my darling?' he said when I went back to the sitting room. He often asked me this and I always said I was even though I wasn't. Poor Derek, he knew the true answer and that I would never give it.

'Can I get you anything?'

'No, you can just come and sit here with me and be my little girl.' He smiled. I tried to.

Since Elizabeth had gone away to college it had been so hard, with just the two of us. Derek had always treated me more like a child than a wife, his two girls, he would say. He liked it best when we were kneeling either side of his chair, something that had started when Elizabeth was a little girl and just never stopped. He would rest his hands on our shoulders, then stroke our hair and one of us would put our head in his lap. The television would always be on and I watched years of it sideways.

I'd been married to Derek twenty-five years. He was old enough to be my father and perhaps that was what I'd wanted as I had never known my own. Mama would never tell me anything about him, not even his name or how they'd met, or how it had ended. I used to envy my sister, who knew who her father was, Mama's husband who had died long before I was born. He'd been nearly eighty when they married. Mama never spoke about him either.

I was a disgrace when I was inside Mama, which was why we left Leicester and came to Ely, where I always felt like an outsider. There are plenty of foreigners there, but they don't look like it, they come from Eastern Europe to work in the fields. I tried that sort of work but I got so cold I thought I would pass out with it and gave up before the summer came.

An indoors job was what I wanted, but as I'd done badly at school I didn't think I'd ever get into an office, so I started cleaning, which I'd always known how to do, and that's how I met Derek.

His house was in a terrible muddle when I started. It was a big old place near the cathedral and not much warmer than being in the fields, but there was such a lot to do I didn't notice so much. He lived there with his mother, who seemed impossibly old to me then. Derek had been in London for a long time but when his mother got frail he moved back to Ely. I admired him for that.

My job was to look after them, even though I was only seventeen. I saw the job advertised in the Cambridge Evening News and didn't think I would get it because of my age, but I don't think anyone else applied. When I went for the interview Derek let me in but it was his mother who saw me. He took me through a dark hallway with a stone floor and into this huge kitchen with a wooden table in the middle and Mrs Rolls sitting there. I was already thinking whether a stone floor would be harder to clean than lino or carpet. Mrs Rolls was looking me up and down.

'D'you think you'll be able to manage this old place, dear?' Her face was as crinkled as a screwed up brown paper bag which had had chips in it, there were patches of grease which caught the light from the kitchen window. She was very nearly bald, had a big pair of sparkly earrings which hung to her jaw and eyes which saw straight through you. I could see, even though she was sitting down, that she was as thin as a bird, one which had already been plucked and drawn. I thought about the fields and shivered.

'Don't be nervous, dear. What's your name again?'

'Simone, madam.'

'That's rather exotic. And it suits you.' She smiled, greenie-yellow teeth like lopsided tombstones. She made me think of death.

Derek, Mr Rolls, was still standing by the door, as if he didn't really want to be involved or perhaps because he wanted to avoid what came next.

'I expect Simone would like a cup of coffee, Derek.'

A moment of inspiration: 'I'll make it, madam. Just tell me where things are.'

I think that did it.

Chapter Fifteen

'Call me "Mrs R", dear,' she said. 'We don't want to be too formal. When can you start? Today?' I didn't like her thinking that I could do this, so I said it would have to be the following week because I had commitments, people I could not let down.

'I like loyalty,' she said. 'Pour me another cup of coffee before you go, will you.'

Over the next few days I scoured the paper looking for something else, but then I started to think I could do worse than look after Mrs Rolls and her son, that I could make the job suit me. So I turned up on the Monday morning, and perhaps there was a little thought that in due course this might be my house and I would be employing someone to look after it.

These were the sort of fantasies that could keep you going when you were cleaning someone else's toilet and scrubbing their grease off the bath, feeling their smell invade you. The only bit of the job I liked was going out to do the shopping. Before going to the supermarket I'd have a look in the clothes shops, try on a few things, and then I'd go to one of the charity shops and buy something. There were always clothes to fit me, small sizes fat women had given up on. Some of them would still have the cardboard labels attached.

I'd stuff whatever I bought at the bottom of one of Mrs R's shopping bags before I went to the supermarket, and when I got back to the house I would unpack everything on the kitchen table and whisk the bag away with the dress or jumper in it before Mrs R could see. I'd put the bags in the cupboard under the stairs where I hung my coat and that made it easy to grab whatever I'd bought just before I went home.

After I'd hung the bags in the cupboard I would go back into the kitchen and Mrs R would watch as I put everything away, telling me if something was in the wrong place, and then I'd make coffee for her and get to work on making the lunch. I got used to her watching me, sitting there at the table, I could feel her eyes on my back. She was a nosey old bag and would keep asking me questions about myself, questions to which there were no satisfactory answers to be given as far as I was concerned, so I deflected them by asking about her. 'Have you always lived in Ely, Simone?' 'For a while. Have you always lived here, Mrs R?' And that would be enough to get her going on how the town had changed, although as she never went out I couldn't see how she knew.

Derek, who had asked me to call him this, not Mr Rolls or Mr R, was mostly in the room he called his study but would come to the kitchen for his lunch. He had his mother's build apart from his belly, which he called his paunch and which he would pat when I offered more soup. 'Got to watch it,' he'd say.

Some days I'd think I'd done everything and perhaps could go home early, but Mrs R would always find something else for me to do, like clean out a cupboard or run the vacuum over somewhere I'd done only the day before. She wanted her money's worth,

I thought, but as time went on I began to think she just wanted to hear something going on in the house. I wondered how old she was. I reckoned Derek was in his fifties, so she could have been in her eighties. The few times she got up from the kitchen table she moved very slowly, like a crow picking its way over a frozen field. Then I'd hear the tinny thump of the old-fashioned lavatory being flushed and she would come back to her perch and continue with some story or other about when she was young. Tennis parties. 'Did I play tennis?' she'd interrupt herself.

Two years I stuck it out, but I suppose it wasn't so bad, no worse than I'd expected. I did the work, avoided as much as possible saying anything about myself, and went home to watch television, there was nowhere in Ely I wanted to go to in the evenings, it was a place with pubs where men drank. There was the cinema, but what was the point when you had the TV.

All this time I felt as if I was waiting for my life to start. My sister had started hers, she'd met a man, although she never brought him home. She said he was too shy, but I didn't believe her. I thought she was probably ashamed of us and our flat and didn't want him to see any of it. She went out twice a week to meet him. Mama would say 'Why don't you bring him home?' and she would shrug and be out the door. Mama would sigh, as if it she was resigned to being not good enough, and I hated my sister for it.

I didn't really concentrate on the television programmes, my head would be full of ways to get away from Ely and finding a better life, but I suppose I was always scared that if I made my escape it would be to something worse. No money, no qualifications, the wrong colour. But it didn't stop me dreaming.

Almost two years to the day from when I started my job I arrived one morning and after letting myself in and going through to the kitchen I found it empty, no Mrs R. Derek came out of his study and told me they'd had a bit of an upset in the night and his mother had gone to hospital. We were standing facing one another. He looked straight at me and added: 'She's dead.'

There was a brief pause during which I was thinking about my job, and then I moved towards him and put my arms round him, a sympathy hug.

Then he began to cry and it developed into big sobs, so I hugged him tighter and tighter, feeling his belly buffeting between us. The mousey smell was almost too much, so I buried my face in his chest. This went on for a while until I felt I couldn't breathe, and gently pulled myself away. I took his hand and guided him to his chair at the kitchen table. There was a pile of ironing to be done and I found a handkerchief for him. He blew into it loudly then sniffed and apologised several times while I busied myself with the kettle.

'A heart attack,' he said.

'Your poor mama,' I heard myself say, trying to think how I would feel if Mama had a heart attack and died. I didn't know. It was not something I had ever thought about.

I stood by the kettle, waiting for it to boil and

thinking about a dress I had seen in the charity shop
and whether I would still be able to buy it.

'She was very fond of you,' Derek said as I placed
a cup and saucer for him on the table. It had never
occurred to me that anyone outside my family could be
fond of me. So I said I was very fond of her too. Then
Derek said he was very fond of me too. I sat down
beside him and he took my hand. I glanced at him,
his sad face which was going to be like his mother's
before too long, his scraggly bits of hair combed over
his bald head. Could I?

'What are we going to do now, Simone? What are
we going to do without her?

Chapter Sixteen

'I'm a lot older than you, Simone,' he began. We were back in the kitchen, the day of the funeral, only the two of us had been there, at the crematorium, watching the curtains slowly moving round to hide the coffin as it began to creep towards wherever it was going. Derek had held on to my hand the whole time. We were the black crows today, coming out into the cold with slow steps that seemed right for the occasion. During the service I did think a bit about Mrs R, her tennis parties, her life which it seemed to me had ended long ago, before all that sitting at the kitchen table. I can't say I felt sad for her, she could have lived a bit more, she had the money, sitting had been her choice.

A choice was coming my way, I could feel it like a heavy heart unavoidably between me and Derek, between me and the rest of my life, well, maybe not that long. I didn't want to look into his face because I knew what I would see and it frightened me a bit, the look of a man who wanted me.

'But because I am that much older, I think it would be alright, there would be no talk.'

I said nothing. We were sitting at the table. I noticed some crumbs and thought about getting up for a cloth, but the moment felt too intense and part of me didn't want to break out of it.

'The thing is Simone, I'm no good on my own, can't look after myself, hopeless, and we rub along together pretty well, don't we. I was thinking, well, I was thinking that you might like to move in and be my full-time housekeeper. There, what do you say?'

There, what do you say? I say nothing because you have just made me feel quite different about myself. I should have studied your face more and then I would have known that what I thought was there was not, and I would not have this uncomfortable feeling I have had so often before, the moments when I know, without anything in particular having been said, that I am discounted, that it should be understood I am a lesser person.

'There's plenty of room here,' he was continuing. 'You could have your own sitting room as well as bedroom, come and go as you please. You know my needs, what the house needs, the same as you've been doing, plus a bit of companionship. What do you say? What do you say?'

And now the hardness in me, the bit I have always relied on to make things bearable. I told him I would think about it. I told him that I had been thinking about taking another job I'd been offered, moving to London. Lies, but he deserved them.

He seemed a bit taken aback, as if he'd assumed I would comply with whatever he wanted, as if it was ungrateful of me to hesitate, to have even considered something else.

I excused myself and went out into the hallway and then I ran upstairs to the bathroom, locked the door and stared at myself in the mirror over the basin. What I saw was ugly. My skin was a sour yellow, my nose too long and flat, "orangutan" they had said at school.

My eyes were too black and not round enough. My mouth was mean and pinched. My hair was black and coarse. I turned away and sat down on the lid of the toilet. Derek did not want me after all. He did not see me in that way, I was other, not someone to love. I had despised him because I thought he felt sorry for himself, and now I despised myself.

I said I'd take the job. Derek, although I am certain he didn't know it, had put me down. I didn't have enough left in me then to refuse his offer or go looking for something else. I wondered what Mama would say, but she probably saw my new position just as Derek did, she told me I was lucky.

There wasn't a lot of stuff for me to pack, and I left behind the childhood things. My sister had more or less left home by that point. She spent most nights at her boyfriend's flat. Mama was going to be on her own but she seemed less anxious about this than I had supposed. There was something about her I had never seen before, a sort of anticipation, even excitement, her way would be clear for whatever it was she had in mind and wasn't telling me.

Derek had given me money for a taxi to bring my stuff to his house. The driver, who looked a bit like Michael Caine, had flirted with me, which gave me a bit of a lift (hah!), so I was feeling more positive about it all by the time I got there. I was lucky. I had a job, a kind enough employer, plenty of time to myself, I could do what I liked really, as long as I kept the house well and provided Derek with his meagre meals during which he would smoke more than eat.

In the evenings I made a point of going out, often just for a walk, along by the river where the boats were moored and sometimes there were parties. I remember one night hearing one going on. I paused and then moved into the shadow of a tree so I could listen for a while. I imagined the people on the boat to be like the ones Mrs R had played tennis with when she was young. I don't know why, the sound of them just made me think of this, and I wanted to eavesdrop for a little while, to try and see if I could get any sort of feel for what their lives were like. I didn't think I wanted to be part of anything like that, I just wanted to know, to imagine how they felt about their lives.

Derek watched TV in the evenings after I'd cleared away supper and some nights, if it was raining or too cold outside, I would sit with him. I'd go to bed when the news came on, but he would stay up until late into the night, not tired enough to go to bed himself, because he didn't do much during the day. He was a lawyer, but I had not seen him doing any work at home and he never went out. He'd had a lawyer's job in London before he'd come back to Ely to be with his mother. He had been too young to retire but that was what he had done and he must have thought there would be enough money from Mrs R to last him out. He'd been wrong about that.

I suppose I relaxed a bit after moving in and knowing I wasn't going to have to sleep with Derek, but I never felt this was going to be my life, it was just a small part of it to be got through until I found whatever it was that would make me happy; and this, as it had been all my life, seemed to be beyond anything I could imagine as possible.

Chapter Seventeen

'Life is what happens while you are making other plans.' I saw this on a postcard in the paper shop one day when I went in to pay the bill for all the newspapers Derek had delivered. It made me feel uncomfortable because I didn't have other plans. Even Mama, when I went to spend an evening with her or watch the wrestling on a Saturday afternoon, had started to ask me. 'What you going to do, Simone? What you going to do with your life?'

'I've no plans, Mama.'

'Well, you should have. Look at your sister, she's got plans.'

'To get married and have children.'

'What's wrong with that?'

'Nothing.'

It was all very well having plans, I thought, but no good if you weren't going to meet a man to make them possible, and I had little chance of that.

I was glad to get away from home and the things Mama said which always sounded disappointed with me. 'I don't know why you keep buying new dresses when you've nowhere to go in them.' 'Why can't you find a decent job with prospects?' 'Why can't you be more like your sister?'

She chipped away at me like this and if I moaned or shrugged she would say it was for my own good.

I stopped going to see her so often, which meant she could add another thing to go on at me about 'why don't you ever come and see me?'

I wondered what she would say if I told her it was because I didn't want to, because she made me feel shrivelled up inside. The best time for me was my nights out, walking through the town and down to the river, listening for the parties on the boats.

Mostly they were quiet and in darkness, but some had lights on and I would try to see inside, I wanted to see people enjoying themselves, to know that it was possible. I suppose it was the same as watching TV soaps, getting caught up in someone else's love affair, getting an idea of how it would feel.

Then one night I got caught. It was very dark, you couldn't see the moon or stars and perhaps I thought I was invisible. A man's head appeared round the door into the boat. My instinct was to run but before I could get going he said 'why don't you come and join us'.

I didn't reply, but after a moment I started going towards him and then I was clambering over the side of the boat and ahead, through the open door, I could see five or six men each holding a tin of beer.

They were all fairly drunk and I felt I had made a mistake, but didn't feel I could just turn and go. They made a place for me to sit and gave me a tin. The man who had let me in pulled the tab on the tin for me and told me to tip it back as there was plenty more.

'Where do you come from, sweetheart?' One of them asked.

'Ely.'

They all laughed.

'Not enough sun here for a skin like yours, darlin.'

I glanced at them. They weren't young, but not old either. One had a long ponytail, another a huge tattoo of a fish on his neck. They were all smoking but whatever it was did not smell like Derek's cigarettes.

Then one of them was giving me a hard look: 'You're not the Old Bill, are you?' The others now looked uneasy. The Old Bill? The Bill, I'd seen that on TV. I shook my head.

'So, Ely girl, what you doing creeping about looking into other people's business?' This was the man with the tattoo.

'I was just going for a walk,' I heard myself say quietly.

'Nosey girl, aren't you.' I didn't answer. It didn't seem to be a question.

A sudden swell from the river buffeted the boat and beer slopped onto the floor. 'Can't waste that,' the man with the ponytail said and knelt to lick it up.

'Ugh, you dog,' one of the others said.

'Come on, now that we have a lady present let's have some music,' said the man who had let me in. I had not looked at him properly until now and it had been so dark outside; but now I realised he was the taxi-driver who had taken me to Derek's. He must have seen the recognition in my expression and smiled. 'Yes, I remember you too.'

He didn't bother to persist with this and turned his back to fiddle with a radio, lots of hissing and snatches of voice, until he found a music station with Motown. This seemed to suit the others and some of them started singing bits, their voices terrible. I was wondering how long it would be before I could leave. I didn't feel at all comfortable and began to think how stupid I was to have thought people on boats would be like people who went to tennis parties, although I didn't actually know what they were like either. And then the man with the tattoo was standing unsteadily in front of me and reaching for my hand. 'Let's dance,' he slurred.

I did as I was told and stood up, starting to hop from one leg to the other, aware there was not much headroom; but the tattooed man grabbed hold of me and began to attempt a smooch. My nose pressed into his shirt I could smell the acrid stench from his armpit. I tried to move away but he had me in a bear hug.

I think the taxi driver must have seen I was not enjoying this, he came up to us, which was not much more than a step in this tight space, tapped my dancing partner on the shoulder and said 'leave her alone, she'll get sea sick'.

I sat down with relief and began to think I probably did feel a bit sick. I had taken one or two sips from the tin, the first time I had drunk alcohol, and the smell of the man I'd been dancing with hadn't helped.

'What's your name Ely girl?' This was another of the men, bald with a big belly.

'Simone.'

'Well, Simone, now that you're here, how about a fry-up? You've got some grub, Baz?' He was talking to the taxi driver, the one I had thought looked a bit like Michael Caine, but now I wasn't so sure. He had the lazy-looking eyes, his hair was blond, his face long, there were similarities, but it was more in the voice.

'If you want to eat you can make it yourself,' he said to the fat one.

'What? With a girlie here?'

'She's our guest.'

The fat man said no more. I was beginning to see the way things were among them. The taxi driver - Michael Caine - Baz, was the one in charge. He spoke softly and spread the words out, but the way he said them made him sound like the boss.

The fat man stood up now and said he was going to get some fish and chips, and the others said they would come with him seeing as how it didn't look as if any grub was going to be on offer on the boat. Swaying and knocking into one another, they took the steps up to the doorway. When they were on the deck I heard a long belch and then an equally long fart. I didn't mean to catch Baz's eye, but the next minute we were both laughing.

'I'll give you a lift home,' he said, 'although perhaps we'll wait for the air to clear before we go up there.'

'Do you live on this boat?'

'It's just a place where me and the boys can drink and smoke what we like.'

I could see more of it now the others had gone. It was not in a good state, it couldn't have been cleaned in a long time. And the curtains which should have covered the window where I'd looked in, were torn and hanging off their pole. The seats were stained and there were cigarette burns. It was nothing like I had imagined the inside of a boat would be. There wasn't the least bit of glamour.

Baz went up the steps first and then turned to take my arm to help me. An odd sensation ran through me, then quickly gone. We walked to the car park round the corner, to his taxi. When we got in I wondered whether he would switch on the meter, but I think I knew he wouldn't. We drove through the quietness of the town. I didn't have to tell him where Derek's house was, he remembered.

Chapter Eighteen

It was late but Derek was still downstairs in the fug-filled room, not so different, I thought, from the boat. What was it people liked so much about smoking? I couldn't see the point of it, all it seemed to do was make everywhere and everything stink. It was there all the time. It would rise up at me when I did the hoovering and plumped up the cushions, and in the daylight I could see a brown circle on the ceiling above Derek's chair.

I'd hear him cough, but not when I was with him, as if he was holding it back out of shame. And I hated emptying his ashtrays, the stink was at its worst, really bad mouse. I'd never had a mouse, but there had been some at school, and when the cage needed cleaning there was this pungent smell. You remember smells.

I knocked on the door downstairs and opened it a crack, just to let him know I was in, although I don't know why I thought I should do this.

'Nice evening?'

'Just a walk.'

'But you enjoyed it.'

'It was alright.'

'Going to bed now, or do you think you might like some coffee?' I knew this meant he wanted me to make some for him.

'Coffee would be nice,' I said, although it was the last thing I wanted. Bed. I was quite tired, and my heart was still pitta-pattering a bit after being on the boat with the men. I suppose I had been a little bit frightened.

When I took the coffee to Derek he had his sad smile on.

'Won't you sit with me for a bit?'

I sat down on the sofa which was at an angle to his chair. He had turned down the sound on the TV.

'Ah,' he said, sipping at his coffee, settling further back into the chair. 'This is nice. You're a good girl, Simone, and I hope I don't take you for granted.'

I wanted to say 'You pay me', but I didn't, because I knew it would have sounded unkind, and I didn't think he really wanted an answer.

'I've been watching this programme,' he started and then began to tell me about it but I wasn't properly listening, I kept thinking about the men on the boat, mostly the taxi driver.

'So you can see why I was interested,' Derek was looking at me. I nodded, and he seemed satisfied.

'I can see you want to go to bed. Sorry if I've kept you up.'

I nodded again.

That night I found it difficult to sleep. I kept thinking about the way I had spent the evening and trying to decide whether I had hated it or liked it.

I couldn't decide, so the following week, on the same day, I went out for a walk again, only this time it was raining by the time I reached the river. I didn't have an umbrella or a hat or anything and I was getting soaked, my hair sticking to my face, but I didn't mind, it gave me a reason.

The rain was making a racket on the boats, too much to hear if there were any sounds coming from inside them. I started to slow up a bit as I got nearer to Baz's, and realised I felt something like disappointment when I saw that it was in darkness. I must have paused for a moment, perhaps to make sure, I don't know what I was thinking. Then I realised that I was now horribly wet and that the rain was getting heavier and faster. I climbed onto Baz's boat and tried the door handle. It wasn't locked. Inside it was pitch black, but I wasn't going to switch on a light even if I could find where it was.

I pulled the door shut as quietly as I could because I knew I should not be here. I went down the steps and felt for somewhere to sit down until I got used to the darkness. The rain on the roof had a different sound from the one it had made outside, as if it desperately wanted to come in and was angry about being shut out. I started to shiver. Then I closed my eyes and tried to see in my mind's eye how it had been when the men were there. The pitter-patter came again. And then I froze as I heard another sound and the boat rocked.

Chapter Nineteen

I was very frightened now. It could be anybody, a total stranger, somebody who was the real owner of the boat. They might think I was a thief, call the police, and then I'd lose my job and not get another one and I'd have to go back to Mama's, although she might not let me, and then I'd have nowhere to go and, and … how can you think so many things in just a fraction of a second?

The light went on and it was Baz. He didn't say anything at first, just looked at me as if he was weighing up the situation, not smiling, not anything, just looking.

I spoke first: 'I got caught in the rain. I hope you don't mind. The door wasn't locked,' I heard myself saying this, although it felt like someone else, and not convincing. I stood up and went to pass him to get to the door, but he put his hand on my shoulder.

'Don't be daft, it's stair rods out there.'

'I'm sorry, I shouldn't be here.'

'But you are, aren't you.'

'It was so, so rainy.'

'I've got a towel somewhere, probably not too clean.' He bent down and opened a cupboard under one of the seats, pulling out a beach towel, faded and torn. He handed it to me and after a moment's pause I began to rub my hair with it but without much effort. I kept looking at him to see if he was angry. Then he grabbed the towel from me and gave my hair a good rub. For a moment I felt like a child, like I had when Mama had washed my hair for me.

When he stopped the rubbing he gently passed the towel over my face, held my gaze for a moment or two then turned away, as if he'd been thinking something and changed his mind.

'When you have dried out I'll take you home,' he said, not looking at me as he said this.

'It's alright,' I heard myself saying. 'I'm already soaked through, so it won't make any difference if I go now.' Then I added: 'I am sorry to have trespassed on your boat.'

'So you should be, Simone. So you should be.' He was looking at me again now and his expression had changed. I couldn't read what he was thinking. I didn't know.

When I found out, it was more than I could ever have imagined. If I had felt there was a big part of my life missing, now I knew what it was. Baz hurt me, but I wanted it to go on and on until there was a sort of explosion in my head and everywhere.

'I think that's what you came for,' he said afterwards, as he lit a cigarette. I didn't answer because I hadn't known, but I suppose he was right.

I got up to put my damp clothes on, keeping my back to his gaze, shy because he seemed to know more about me than I did myself. The light was dim, but not enough that I couldn't see a patch of blood on the place where I had been. Baz followed my gaze, the cigarette between his lips. For a moment he looked at me with a sort of tenderness, almost apologetic.

Then he smiled at me: 'It's nice to be the first.'

I looked at his body now, feeling I had the right. I also realised the sound of the rain had gone. I took a step or two up to the door, opened it a crack and could see the night had become clear. I turned to him again. I said I would go now, that I didn't need a lift home, that I was alright. He made a half-hearted attempt to rouse himself, then slumped back, lifting his hand in a brief wave.

'Come again,' he called to me as I closed the door behind me.

They say you feel different. I don't really understand that. I just felt as if I had made a huge discovery, a sensation I had found so intoxicating and could not have imagined until it happened. All the way home I thought about it, over and over. My mind was not focused on Baz, only on what he had done.

The next morning Derek asked me if I was alright. He was sitting at the kitchen table, watching me make his breakfast. I could feel his eyes on me as I went from cupboard to cupboard, was it possible that he sensed something different about me?

'Why do you ask?'

'I just like to know that you are happy.'

'Happy?'

'Well, content. Content is a good place to be, Simone. It can lead to being happy.'

I had no idea what he was on about, but I didn't think it had anything to do with what had happened to me on the boat.

'I'm happy and content,' I said, without considering whether I was either.

'That's alright then. I worry sometimes Simone, that I am being selfish keeping you here to look after me. You're so young. Sometimes I think you should be off making your way in life, having a good time, being with people your own age.'

Now I was worried. Was he working up to giving me the sack? On impulse I went over and kissed him on the cheek. Suddenly he seemed like a wrinkled child who had been waiting for a bit of affection. We looked at each other and I saw the neediness in him. Poor Derek, I hadn't thought how much he must be missing his mother. I decided he wasn't going to sack me, but at the same time something triggered inside me, what he had said about making my way in life, and I knew I would have to move on before long, that I did have to try and make a life better than this.

Chapter Twenty

I had begun to look in the jobs pages of the Cambridge Evening News, but without any qualifications there was not much I could go for, until I saw that one of the colleges wanted what they called 'bedders', people to make students' beds and clean their rooms. I thought about this for a while and it began to seem like a good opportunity, to get away from Ely and to be with people my own age, even if all I was doing was making their beds. Several evenings after what had happened with Baz I took a walk along the river but the boat was always in darkness. One time I looked to see there was no one about then stepped onto the boat and tried the door, but it was locked. So I stopped going and that was one of the reasons I wanted to leave Ely.

The day the letter came from the college was also the day I realised I was pregnant. I had opened it and saw it was inviting me to go for an interview but in that moment I felt horribly sick and had to dash from the kitchen. When I came back, Derek was sitting at the table, the letter in front of him.

He didn't look at me. He said: 'Of course, I shall give you an excellent reference.' Then I saw there was a tear rolling down his sunken cheek, and somehow that made me do the same. I sat down beside him and we both sat there crying.

'You don't really want to leave, do you?'

Yes, I wanted to say, I do want to leave but now I can't, or not until it shows, and then you will probably throw me out and I shall have to go back to Mama's and my life will be miserable and I'll never escape from Ely. Then I felt sick again and had to run for the door.

By the time I came back I realised that this was going to be how it would go on, being sick all the time, and that I might as well get it over with and tell him straight out.

'I think I'm pregnant.'

He didn't say anything at first, but his tears had stopped. He sniffed, took out a handkerchief I had ironed the night before and blew heavily into it. All I could think of in that moment was the snot I would try not to see when I did the washing. An involuntary shiver of disgust went through me. And now Derek had reached for my hand.

'I suppose this means you'll be leaving to get married. Who is the lucky chap? Does he live in Cambridge? Is that why you have been looking for a job there?'

I shook my head. I didn't want to tell him about Baz. I didn't want him to know that I had been looking for another job because I wanted another job, no other reason. I didn't want to hurt him, he had done nothing to deserve it, he had always been nice to me.

'I am not getting married,' I said quietly, too quietly.

'What did you say?'

'I am not getting married. I expect you would like me to leave. I'm sorry. Perhaps I should go and pack my things.' But as I stood up he reached for my hand again, this time grabbing hold of it.

'Don't go, Simone. Stay here. Have your baby. I've often thought it would be nice to have a child about the place. Stay here as long as you like, there's plenty of room for three of us. Stay, please stay.'

'But what will it look like? I mean, what will your neighbours think?'

'Bugger the neighbours. Bugger the lot of them.' He was sounding well made up now, as if it was all about him. But that wasn't fair of me, not fair on this kind man who wanted to help me. Regretting this mean thought, I kissed him again on the cheek.

'Simone. Do you know what would make me really happy? Do you know what I might always have hoped for but never thought remotely possible?'

Derek and I got married before the baby started to show. We went to the register office one afternoon after I had stopped being sick. Derek had asked his solicitor to be a witness and the solicitor had brought along his secretary to be the other. Both seemed as if they would prefer to be doing something else and left as soon as the ceremony was over, saying they were sorry but had to get back to the office.

Derek said we should at least go to a pub to celebrate and as I didn't feel sick in the afternoons, I agreed. He bought a bottle of champagne. I took a sip to please him, but I didn't like the taste. I sat still and quiet beside him and felt completely lost, numb, I think, too. Even though there was something living inside me, something had died. I tried not to think about the rest of my life with Derek. I tried not to think at all.

Telling my mother and sister was going to be the next thing. They would be angry with me for not inviting them to the wedding, but I had not wanted them there. It would have felt more real if they had been.

At the weekend I told Derek I would go and see them, planning to go by myself, but he insisted on coming with me, and I could see that it would be unreasonable to say no.

'I thought as much,' Mama said when I told her about the baby. 'Last time you came to visit.'

She gave Derek one of her long, penetrating looks, as if trying to decide whether or not to be nice to him; but at the same time I could see she was a bit in awe of him. I don't suppose she ever imagined me marrying a solicitor.

My sister was offhand with us, but I think that was mainly because I had got married before she had.

We didn't stay very long. The atmosphere was stiff, with Mama being put out by us not inviting her to the wedding and having been denied her opportunity to have a go at me about the baby. I could see the frustration in her expression and I felt good about that. For once I had thwarted her. I didn't really care what my sister thought.

Back at the house, things went on exactly as before. The night of the wedding Derek had gone to his sitting room and turned on the telly. I went in and sat with him for a bit, but I was tired, so I said goodnight and went to my room. I lay down on the bed and immediately fell asleep, waking an hour or so later. The house was quiet. I took off my clothes and got under the covers. I wondered whether Derek was expecting me to go to his room, or whether he might come to mine. I suppose I lay awake for a while, listening.

In the morning, after being sick a few times, I managed to make breakfast and even sit and watch him eat it. When he'd come downstairs into the kitchen he had given me a kiss on the forehead before sitting at the table, waiting to be served.

'Did you sleep well, Mrs Rolls?' This gave me a bit of start, all I could think of was his mother, the real Mrs Rolls. And that got me thinking about what she would have thought about her son marrying someone like me.

Chapter Twenty-One

Nick

It was a difficult time for me. I had not thought that C would leave. I thought she had more sense than that. I even said to her it was a pity she'd found out as it would probably have fizzled out. That was what had happened in the past, although those affairs had all been short-lived. It was different with Simone, even though I had never intended it to be.

The first time I met her I thought I had made another mistake, like the fat woman, fatter than C, who I'd arranged to meet, where I nearly always met them, at the hotel in Huntingdon. Then there had been the one who wanted someone to spend weekends with, I told her she was on the wrong dating site; but she was a good-looking woman and I was tempted to suggest we take a room for the afternoon. I decided against because there was something too needy about her and that could lead to trouble.

It was the best part of a year before C found out. I'm not sure whether or not I wanted her to know, although once she did, it was a relief to be able to talk to her about Simone. The night C found out I was still in two minds whether to tell her; after all, she'd bought what I'd said the previous week, after the night away. Then she wanted us to talk about the future, spending more time together, going out on jaunts, she hadn't a clue. She wanted us to each make lists of things to do, the sort of stuff I hadn't minded in the past, in the days when I wanted her all the time. We used to go to National Trust houses, gardens open to the public, all of it boring, I couldn't see the point. All those pictures of people looking as bored as they were boring. C said they were Huguenots, I thought of them as huge noses, and it might have been because of that I spotted there was something not quite right about C's nose. It didn't quite fit her face, and then I saw a photo from long before I'd known her and her nose was different. She'd had an operation, not cosmetic, something to do with breathing problems, a bone had been removed from the bridge. The only way I can describe what I thought was that it was like getting a new car and then finding out it had been tampered with, damaged, resprayed, and after that you never feel the same again about it.

I'm not sure when I stopped loving C, but I loved her very much at the beginning, I must have done to leave my family to be with her, although I was bored with my first marriage, I had been looking around. Even so, I had not planned to leave, just have a bit of fun on the side, which I had managed quite well with the women before C.

C was not that good-looking, I didn't think so at first. She was a bit drab, I suppose, but then I started to see potential, if she dressed differently, changed her hair. What I liked most was her voice, it was so posh, she was going to be a step up, the sort of woman who would suit me well.

Things were going well when I first met her. The

business was growing, I had some good staff and the plan was to move to a bigger factory, raise our game, perhaps even float on the stock market in a few years. My first wife was working in the business and that's how she found out about C. I'd booked an hotel room, my first wife was part time in the accounts department. Perhaps she was suspicious anyway, and, as with C all these years later, I was not as careful as I might have been.

I'd made the booking myself and put it through the books as an overnight stay for someone visiting the company. It would have gone unnoticed if Marion hadn't already been looking for evidence. There had been no visitors that week.

It was a bad time for me. Marion was upset, of course, kept saying she didn't know why she loved me so much. I didn't want to say I didn't love her, but in the end I had to, it seemed to me the only way she could move on. Then she told me she'd once thought about leaving me, someone she worked with. That made me feel better about going off with Charlotte.

The first person outside it all that I told was my co-director Barry. If he was in we'd often have a drink in my office after everyone else had gone home. We'd talk about the business, make plans, the money was tight but we reckoned we were on a roll, we'd re-invented plimsolls as trainers and everyone was starting to want them.

For once, Barry, king of the salesman's patter, didn't say anything. Perhaps he thought I could have done better, perhaps I could, but I was dead set on

Charlotte by then. I had to have her.

She had been doing some freelance writing for us, press releases, articles. She didn't know what she was doing at first, but she listened to me and started to get it right.

"You have to sell the sizzle, not the sausage," I told her, and she got it. I don't think I could have gone off with her if she hadn't.

After everybody knew about us and we'd moved in together I took her shopping, bought her some new clothes, and I had a go at her hair myself. She looked so much better.

I suppose she started to irritate me fairly early on. She'd disagree with something I said and then she would complain about my "tone", and we'd have an argument about that.

Fairly early on there was a bad episode. I'd taken her with me on a business trip to Germany. I'd driven there and we were in a hotel on the way back. We'd had one of those arguments in the car and she'd gone quiet. In the hotel room she was sitting on the side of the bed and there was something different about her, she seemed to be distancing herself from me. Then she told me she didn't think she could go on, that she felt as if she had gone off me.

I thought very quickly about all my options, go back to Marion, start looking again for someone else, but I wasn't ready to let her go, I had become obsessed by her, or what I had perceived to be her, and I still wanted her all the time. Besides, I was not prepared to be dumped.

I sat down beside her and took her hand. For a moment I thought she was going to snatch it away, but she let me hold it, even if with no response.

"You're just missing your daughter," I said, quietly.

She didn't answer, and I knew I had a selling job on my hands.

"You don't just stop loving someone." This, of course, was not true, but it seemed like a good line to take.

What I wanted was to get her talking because the best-selling technique is to listen.

She must have started, although I don't remember what she said, only that the trick worked and later that night things were back on course.

Chapter Twenty-Two

'I think we need to change your name,' I said to her soon after her wobble at the hotel. 'As soon as we are both divorced, I think we should get married.'

I don't remember what she said, but she must have agreed. I wanted to get things sorted out so that I could concentrate on the business, and on Barry. I felt that the company had outgrown him and it was going to be only a matter of time before I had to get rid of him. He had become a buffoon, and the more the business thrived the worse he got, big-timing in front of the staff, constantly speaking in clichés, I dreaded to think what he was like with our customers.

A big wedding did not seem appropriate, and I didn't want to spend the money, everything was being ploughed back into the business at this stage. The biggest expense was buying the wedding rings; when we went to buy hers I saw one I liked, so we bought two.

We had just six guests, her parents, Barry and Pam, and our first friends as a couple, Jane and David.

Charlotte's parents had not much cared for her first husband, they thought he neglected their daughter in favour of sport, which he did; I don't think she would have been up for an affair otherwise. Her father had demonised him further, implying that he was a gambler. Charlotte never said he was, though.

I don't remember much about the day we got married. It was hot, and my suit felt uncomfortable, but more to the point, I was worried about the business, we were perilously close to overtrading.

We went through the ceremony at the register office and then on for lunch, the same hotel where Charlotte and I had first had sex.

The lunch was a farce. Charlotte's father, a crusty old chap, sent his food back twice, made a fuss, as if he was paying for it.

"If your chef can't cook a steak, I'll have the chicken." I remember him saying that and the waitress looking as if she would spit on his plate before it came out again. I hope she did. God, he turned out to be pain, that man.

The occasion wasn't helped by Jane making sure she sat next to me, having too many glasses of wine and running her hand along my thigh under the table. I'd slept with her a couple of times and she seemed to think this gave her some sort of right to be over-familiar. I don't know whether David noticed, or even cared; she'd told me he was up to the same thing. Everyone was then, there didn't seem to be any reason not to, if it was available you were a fool to turn it down.

Charlotte was sitting on my other side and I think she noticed the way Jane was behaving but perhaps just put it down to the booze.

What else do I remember about that day? Barry's wife Pam, who was to have her own ill-advised fling, was wearing a see-through dress and no bra, and Charlotte's father couldn't keep his eyes off her. Pam was a pea brain and wouldn't have seen that she was dressed inappropriately. She had a sour face but a good body, although I'd put her off limits. Barry referred to her as "it" when he talked about her.

I think I must have made a speech, and then Barry stood up and said that Norman, Charlotte's father, had shown that the customer was king. Shut up, Barry.

It wasn't a good time to be away from the business but I took Charlotte to Venice. It was a good choice. After landing at the airport we walked from the plane to a water taxi to take us into the city. Charlotte loved it, this romantic entrance into the Grand Canal. We went again, years later, with Sophie, and it wasn't the same, buses instead of boats, that first feeling of romance had gone.

The honeymoon was okay. We spent a lot of time in the room, a lot of sex, I'd have been fed up if it hadn't been like that; after all, I'd given up a hell of a lot for her. We walked around the city a fair bit, narrow old streets, unexpected bridges. Then we'd sit in St Mark's Square, order coffee and listen to an orchestra. I could see that C loved every bit of it, except for a pain she kept getting in her chest. I could see when she'd got it, her face would go grey. It also meant she couldn't eat much, and although it was a waste to send away plates of food which had just been picked at, I didn't mind too much, at least she wasn't going to get fat.

The pain persisted and months later I went with her to hospital for an endoscopy, but when the medics tried to get her to swallow the tube she got into a state and they had to put her out to do it. I felt sorry for her, it's not good to be out of control.

I still loved her a lot then, even when she irritated me by going on about my 'tone'. It would start with something trivial, I'd tell her she was wrong but she wouldn't accept it, and then she'd bring up the tone thing, which was rubbish. Sometimes she'd get upset and I'd despise her and want her at the same time.

We agreed fairly early on that we would never have post mortems after an evening out with other people. We wouldn't criticise one another for things either of us had said, although there was one time when we had been to a dinner party and one of the other guests had started talking about his time in the army. It was gung-ho stuff and I thought he was a twit, a stuffed-shirt public schoolboy who had achieved nothing other than what had been handed to him on a plate.

"Nick was in the army," Charlotte piped up. I could have throttled her. I knew what was coming next. Which regiment, what rank? I can't remember what I said to avoid answering, but the other guests were too interested in themselves to push it, although I thought stuffed-shirt's wife gave me an odd look, or perhaps she just fancied me.

"Never again mention that I was in the army," I said to Charlotte on the way home.

"Why not?"

"Because I wasn't an officer, and people like that lot tonight judge you on what you have been rather than what you have become."

"D'you really think so?"

"I know so."

"But does it matter what they think?"

"You don't understand."

"I do, but I don't think you should care."

"I don't care."

"So, why are you going on about it?"

"Don't be stupid."

"Oh, here we go."

That used to annoy me: 'Here we go.'

Charlotte was always too friendly and open with other people. Sometimes I'd be watching her when we were with a group and I could have punched her stupid face.

Chapter Twenty-Three

"You always want other people," I said to her one time when we were on a skiing holiday, just the two of us, that was until we bumped into someone we knew who was with a crowd.

I said this to her when the others were there and the woman we already knew overheard. I think she was tuned into me anyway, there had been the beginnings of something between us at a party a few months earlier. I hadn't pursued it because the business was demanding all of my time. I suppose I'd sort of put her on the back burner, and perhaps she resented this.

"Be nice to Charlotte," she said, which was as insulting to C as it was to me. Charlotte said nothing, but I could see it made her feel uncomfortable, nobody wants other people to see into your relationship like that; but it was her own fault, she was the one who had ruined the holiday.

And she was still getting that pain of hers, even though the hospital had found nothing. Time after time we'd go out for something to eat and she would hardly touch it. I began to think it was all in her mind and if she wasn't careful she'd become like my mother, years and years of thinking she'd got cancer until she got it; but my mother was an unhappy person.

I should not have gone skiing, the business was not where I wanted it to be and leaving Barry in charge was like lending your car to a boy racer, he'd either stall it or crash it.

The night we got home I called him; if there were nasty surprises awaiting my return to the office, I wanted to know about them in advance.

"Good time? Broken anything? You've started something now. It wants to go skiing. Says It wants to get a sun tan." Barry's banter was doubtless a delaying tactic.

"Nothing broken this end. How have things been?"

"Oh, you know, up and down."

This meant mostly down.

"We had a bit of bother with the bailiff."

"What!"

"He seemed to think we hadn't paid the rent on the factory."

"That's nonsense."

"That's what I told him."

"And?"

"Well, he took a few things."

"Such as?"

"Machinery."

"And you let him?"

"Couldn't do much to stop him, chief. He had some big bone heads with him."

"What's happened to production?"

"That's a tricky one."

"Why didn't you phone me?"

"Didn't want to spoil your holiday."

"Christ, Barry, you've spoilt it now."

I'd been pretty sure the landlord would hold off for a few more months, I'd spent enough time explaining our situation. Now it looked as if we were not even going to get the chance to trade out of it. No machinery, no production. God, Barry was such a wimp, and the staff, had they just let it happen? Didn't they want to keep their jobs? Bunch of losers.

"This is all we need," I said to C after I'd suggested to Barry that we both be in by 7am.

I told her what had happened while we'd been away. She listened quietly, perhaps she was in shock, but then she said: "We'll manage. I don't mind being poor with you." She hadn't the first clue about what it was like to be poor.

During the time we were telling each other about our lives, that early part of a relationship when you need to catch up on each other's past, I had told her about the dog, I said it was my dog. I told her how my stepfather had it put down, left it at that, intimating what a heartless bastard he had been, but the truth was we couldn't afford to feed it. I wondered what she would have done if I'd said her golden retriever had to go.

Barry's ebullience was a thin veneer the following morning, I could see he was shit scared, but whether it was of me or what would happen to the business, probably both.

We went into my office and shut the door, the factory workers would be in soon, I didn't want any interruptions, all of them looking to me to sort things out, save their bloody jobs, none of them would think about me, what I stood to lose. They were all so selfish, and that included Barry.

"How could you let things get in such a mess?" I

said, having decided to take the offensive position. "I was only away for a week."

"Sorry, chief." The veneer had gone now and momentarily I felt sorry for him, taking the blame. There again, if I had not had him round my neck all these years it might have been a different story. I'd carried him and now I was paying the price. Before long I'd have to go out to the factory floor and speak to the staff. I had to think of something, a way round it all, but nothing sprang to mind at this moment. The thought of the factory, quiet, unproductive, I hated it. I was sure of one thing, if C hadn't wanted us to go skiing, if I had not been away, then none of this would have happened.

"I think it's better if you go and speak to the staff. Tell them I'll have a word later."

"What shall I tell them?"

"I don't know. You're the one who was here. Tell them I'm trying to sort it out. Tell them to tidy up the place if they've got nothing better to do."

I watched Barry go, a classic exit, opening the door as quietly as possible, looking out into the corridor before he slipped through the gap.

Coffee. I needed coffee. The machine I had bought for my office needed water. Shit! I thought for a minute, looked at my watch. The staff would not be here yet. I grabbed the glass jug and went to the kitchen to fill it. Just as I'd finished, I heard someone in the corridor, so waited to see if they would go straight past the kitchen.

"Oh, hello." It was Sheila, factory supervisor. She looked embarrassed, didn't know what to say.

"Good holiday?" I don't think this was sarcastic, but I didn't answer.

"Look, I'm going to do everything I can to get things going again. Bang on nine-o-clock I'm going to start making calls. But I'll need everybody to keep positive."

Sheila moved towards me and touched my arm. She didn't say anything, just looked at me with pity and then something like hope.

The calls I made were a waste of time. I thought I was getting somewhere with the bank, but realised after a few minutes that the decision had already been made.

It was too dreadful a day to dwell on. After we'd sent everyone home, there was not much that could be done. Sheila insisted on staying, so it was just me and Barry and her, in my office, getting through jugs of coffee, going over the unfairness of what had happened, trying to make some sort of sense of it, see a future. Even while we were going over the past, I was thinking about what next. There was only one sensible option, go into the PR business which Charlotte had started after a lot of pushing from me. I'd take it to a much higher level, really put some welly behind it.

When it began to get dark I got the booze out, the other two seemed in no hurry to leave. I imagined that Barry was terrified of going home and having to tell Pea-brain she was going to have to cancel her spa membership; and Sheila lived alone, the factory had been her life.

We carried on drinking until I wondered how I was

going to drive home.

"Coffee. We need more coffee."

"Why don't you come back with me and I'll make some at home," Sheila said, her speech a little slurred.

"I'm going home to face It," Barry said, stumbling as he got up. "Might as well get it over with."

"Come on, my darling," Sheila said after he'd gone. She'd called me that once on the factory floor, in front of everyone, and I'd reprimanded her for it, over-familiar, but now there was a sort of comfort in it.

Sheila's house was close by. Together we locked up the factory and offices, although god knows why we bothered, then walked along a deserted street to her place, an old cottage, freezing inside. I'd been there before, once or twice. There was a pervasive smell of old cooking fat which had put me off going more often, but I was fond of Sheila and she always made the best of herself. Too much make-up but the effort was there, and her hair changed colour every few months. Her skin was heavy and the make-up on her cheeks had sunk into it in an unappealing way. She was quite a bit older than me and had a sanguine air about her, as if nothing really mattered that much because she'd seen it all and expected little.

I liked sex with her because she came so easily, unlike C, who was hard work. On the way home I swerved when I tried to sniff my sleeve to see how much it had absorbed the cooking fat smell.

When I got in, C came into the hallway looking concerned.

"It's been the most bloody awful day," I said. "We've lost the business." She stared at me for a moment, then came forward and put her arms round me. If she detected the fat smell, she didn't say anything.

Chapter Twenty-Four

I still loved C then. I loved her for a long time and I'm not sure when it stopped, or turned into something else. When her pain went and she started to put on weight, I don't think I noticed straightaway. I remember the moment I registered it. We were at her cousin's house, we went there every Boxing Day, a family party, all his wife's family, the brothers and sisters and their partners and children. You wouldn't have believed that C and her cousin shared grandparents, Clive was proudly coarse, spoke with a broad Suffolk accent, his favourite adjective beginning with "f".

But he put on a good party. He was loaded, made his money from demolition, got what little education he had from Borstal; he was sharp.

And spiteful.

That year, as we were leaving the party, C hugged him and said something like there was a nice lot to hug. "You've put on a lot of weight yourself," he said. And that's when I really saw it, how fat C had become and how it didn't suit her.

That pain of hers had been a blessing, it had kept off the weight. I think it had stopped after she had Sophie, although immediately afterwards she had been incredibly thin, gorgeous really. I think I loved her the most then. And she had given me Sophie.

We'd been together ten years when we had Sophie. Not planned, not at all. I assumed she would want an abortion, like the previous time. That had been a couple of years before we found out she was pregnant again. I always thought she had rushed into that abortion, we had not discussed it, and I had too much going on to realise it could happen so quickly. She got a taxi back from the hospital and when I saw her, looking so relieved, it suddenly dawned on me that she had got rid of my baby. I could hardly speak to her. I thought she was a selfish bitch.

I think she knew what I felt, she couldn't be that unaware; although there had been so many times when I'd wondered whether she had an inkling of what might be going on and chose not to notice.

That night, after she'd come back from what she had done, we argued. It wasn't about the baby, it was the usual nonsense, my 'tone', it could have been about anything, these rows came out of nowhere; the trouble was, she'd never admit when she was wrong. And that night she did one of her disappearing acts, ran out of the house and went god knows where. She was gone for several hours and perhaps I should have been concerned, but I knew it was just point-making and better not indulged. She'd come back.

When she left, she had been crying. I hated that. If a woman couldn't get her own way, that's what she did. And if they thought it would soften my heart, well, it did the opposite. I'd seen my mother doing it, looking for sympathy when none was deserved; she'd married that bozo, nobody had made her. Then, when she did eventually get cancer, she adopted a martyred pose which I found utterly nauseating. I left it to my brother to do the duty visits, she'd always favoured him, it was pay-back time.

I've always said it's better not to think about things too much, by which, of course, I mean the bad things. There's no point, you can't change what's gone wrong, like the business going bust. If I'd been there, if C hadn't made me go skiing, it might have been different, but things had gone too far by the time I got back. Barry had fouled up big time – that man was such a loser, even It left him. And the good times, you don't really dwell on them, they just happen and are okay, it's the bad times you have to make an effort to forget, and most of those involve some kind of rejection.

I became good at seeing the possibility of this coming and heading it off. I could do it when I was selling, which I learnt early on was all about listening. But the most likely area for rejection was sex, and I couldn't tolerate that. I knew C didn't want sex as often as she should, but I found it almost impossible to initiate things, it had to come from her. So, I'd touch her hand when we were in bed, just a light touch, so I could satisfy myself that it was merely that, an indication of affection, if nothing else happened, except it always did. And C always did her best, but I'm afraid there came a time when that wasn't enough.

We still had sex but I was starting to go off her. There are moments you remember as triggers for making clear what has been festering. We were away for a weekend, a friend's birthday party. C had booked a hotel, not nice, but cheap. The party had been a lunchtime affair, dragging on into the evening. Jane was there with her now third husband but that hadn't stopped her making sure she sat next to me at lunch and did the old leg touching act. I didn't mind, I was fond of her, and C never noticed, or chose to ignore anything she did see.

That night, C came out of the bathroom with a ridiculously small towel which covered little of her, and it was then I saw how revoltingly fat she had become. Her thighs were all cellulite, how could she let herself go like this? It was an insult.

I realised I had not seen her naked for some while, and now that I did, I wished I hadn't. She scurried round the bed and got in beside me. We switched out the bedside lights and in the darkness I tried to stop seeing that orange peel texture but it just loomed larger in my mind, revolting. I knew she expected us to have sex so I started trying to imagine she was Simone, but it wasn't working. She had climbed on top of me and I was feeling nothing other than a sense of being smothered.

Then I said it: 'I can't do this.'

The moment I said it, something in me wished I hadn't, but another part wanted this to be the opening for what might become inevitable. 'I can't do this.' Surely she would ask why? But she didn't, she just kissed me and rolled away onto her side of the bed where she immediately lay still and nothing more was said.

Chapter Twenty-Five

I had not thought of Tony as a threat. C quoted him a lot, but she worked with him all day so this was hardly surprising, I don't think she would have mentioned him at all if there had been anything going on.

But that summer, the year before it all blew up, I began to resent C's fondness for him; besides, I did not really believe it was possible for a man and a woman to be friends without anything else, not unless the man was gay. Was Tony gay? I didn't think so, but he did seem to have the sort of empathy with women that gays have. I dismissed him as a mild irritant.

Then C let it go too far. On a couple of occasions I arranged to meet her in town on a Saturday after she had finished shopping, and both times she was with Tony. For Christ's sake, she saw him all week. On both occasions he carried on sitting there, at the café, and it was impossible not to clock how animated C was in his presence. What the hell was going on?

We were in separate cars. I got home first and, failing to follow my own advice, allowed myself to think about C's behaviour. When we were first together, she had said we could never trust one another completely because we had run off together, betrayed our previous partners; I hadn't thought about this for years but now it came into my head and I couldn't get rid of it.

I went into my study with the idea of looking through some work but I couldn't concentrate. I heard

C come in, heard her speak to the cats, listened to her moving between rooms until suddenly I'd had enough. I went out into the hallway, she was coming out of the kitchen.

'You're always with Tony.'

She looked at me and I could see that she was puzzled.

'What do you mean?'

'What I say.'

'Don't be ridiculous.'

'I don't see him as a threat.' I didn't know where that came from but because C had made me say it, I hated her in that moment, so that when she came towards me and tried to put her arms round me, I shrugged her off and went back into the study, closing the door.

It was a Saturday, the night we always had sex, and that night it was like the early days, after we'd had a row, intensity with an edge of dislike.

C looked good that summer. She had been on a diet that involved powders instead of plates of food and she had done well, but of course it didn't last, her dieting efforts never did, not since her pain had gone.

It wasn't long after that particular Saturday she started to send me strange emails which she said were supposed to make me laugh. They were sent to her at work and came from a dating site called Illicit Encounters. I suppose they might have been mildly amusing, but it crossed my mind that she could be telling me something.

I didn't do anything at first but things add up in

your mind, the latest diet, Tony, C sending these emails to me. I thought I'd have a look. And that's how it started. It was C's fault.

I very nearly knocked it on the head after the first few encounters. The women I met were stupid, boring, none of them looked like the photos they'd sent, and within minutes of meeting them, it was clear they wanted more than sex. I suppose I had imagined they would be detached in the same way I was because both of us would be otherwise attached and it was going to be purely physical; but it wasn't at all like that, these women were desperate for affection. I could also see the danger in this, and I didn't want that.

But once you have started doing this sort of thing, it is difficult to leave it alone, and by the time I saw Simone's posting on the site, I was pretty well hooked. I just had to be careful.

'*Simone. 38. Asian. Cambridgeshire.*' That's all it said. I responded. She was 30 years younger than me, but perhaps she had taken a few years off, just as I had. We exchanged photographs. We arranged to meet.

So far, so good, but I always had this dread they might not turn up, even though every single one of them had to date. I was still using the same hotel in Huntingdon although as I drove there this time, it occurred to me that I was going there too often and hotel staff who had nothing much to do other than stand around might start clocking what was going on, not that it was any of their business, but the last thing I wanted was to be recognised, greeted as a regular customer. What would the women think?

If I'd had a phone number for Simone, I would have called her and suggested somewhere else to meet, but I hadn't thought about it until I was nearly there, and communication with her so far had been online. Whatever happened today, I would not meet any more women at the same hotel.

The day was freezing, I remember that, also that the hotel car park was empty. This should not have been surprising, it was 3 o'clock midweek. All of this added up to a sort of bravado I was not feeling, I had become careless and realising this made me uneasy. I wondered whether it might be possible to get a quick look at Simone without her seeing me and if she didn't look up to much, I could make a hasty retreat.

Chapter Twenty-Six

Simone

I arrived late. I had reached Huntingdon early and found a café to sit in. I wanted him to be at the hotel first, so I could see him and decide, although I didn't know the hotel, whether it would be possible to see without being seen.

The photo he had sent me was a bit fuzzy, some men did this on purpose because they knew they were not attractive. In the days since it had arrived, I had looked at it several times, trying to decide if this man was worth the risk. I'd had so many responses since I'd gone on the dating site, far too many. If the people who ran the site had wanted pictures, I don't think this would have happened. After work I had gone to the public library to look through the daily messages. Some of the men wrote vulgar things, wanted me to do stuff I could hardly imagine. I decided to meet Nick because his messages were always polite and I thought he sounded as lonely as I was.

It was so cold the day I met him, by the time I got to the hotel I couldn't stop shivering and realised he would probably think I was nervous, which I was.

It was stupid of me to think I wouldn't be noticed, Nick spotted me straightaway. I thought he looked a lot older than his photo, but it was too late to escape now. My mind was racing, would it be possible to just have a cup of tea, would he turn nasty, follow me, if I said I didn't want to sleep with him?

He was sitting on a sofa by an open fire and the heat drew me. He stood up when I reached him and when he smiled I saw that he was attractive.

'I thought you might have changed your mind,' he said, glancing at his watch, which I noticed looked expensive.

'Not yet.' He seemed to find this amusing.

'How long can you stay?'

'I don't know.'

'Come on. You must have some idea.'

'It depends on you. I haven't done this before.'

'Neither have I.' As he said this, he touched my hand. We were sitting side-by-side now. A waiter came over and asked us whether we would like a drink.

'I don't drink,' I said, without thinking. Had the waiter seen Nick touch my hand? I was beginning to feel hot, the fire was strong.

'We'll have tea.'

'Cakes?' the waiter asked. I couldn't imagine being able to eat a thing.

'My wife drinks too much,' Nick said after the waiter had gone. I realised he was making it clear from the start that there was a wife. I thought about mentioning Derek but I couldn't. All the way here on the train I had being doing my best not to think about Derek.

'I have never drunk alcohol and never smoked.'

'And I don't think you have eaten much cake.' As he said this he was looking at my body.

'Chocolates, though.'

He smiled and touched my hand again, then said something about liking very dark, bitter chocolate himself. I was thinking about whether I wanted to sleep with him. I decided that I did, and was fairly sure he wanted the same.

'What else do you like?'

I wondered whether this was what Derek called 'a loaded question'.

'I like to travel but I haven't been able to much.'

We were silent for a moment or two, one of those silences that is full of things to say.

'What do you like?'

He didn't answer straightaway. Then he looked at me with a steady gaze and said: 'You.'

Derek would have laughed at that.

I don't remember drinking the tea, only that Nick left me alone for quite some time until I thought maybe he had gone, which gave me a sudden cold feeling. I moved nearer the fire and started to wonder how much they charged for tea in a place like this, as I might have to pay if Nick had left.

When he reappeared I felt a huge sense of relief, and I'm not talking about paying for the tea. He walked towards me and put his hand out in a gesture which told me to get up, which I did and followed him out to the lobby and up the wide staircase with its thick, soft carpet, my eyes down for fear of looking round and seeing everyone below looking at me and of course, knowing.

Nick led me along a corridor then stopped outside one of the doors. He had a plastic card which he pushed into a slot but it didn't work at first, and, almost as if I wasn't there, he started cursing. This was not going well. I was about to touch his arm and suggest we leave it but then a small green light came on above the slot and the door opened.

It was a nice room, big heavy curtains which Nick went over to and partially closed, for which I was grateful. I felt nervous now. I knew my body was in good shape but what about his, he looked okay in his clothes, but they could be hiding all sorts of things, and he was old. I should have chosen a man younger than me, after all these years I didn't want disappointment.

In the half-light I took off my clothes but I was too shy to be completely naked. I got into bed with my bra and pants still on and closed my eyes. I listened to the sound of him unbuckling his belt, heard the pull and stretch of his clothes coming off. The bed was cold and I was shivering again.

I kept my eyes closed as he got in beside me and felt his hand touch me. He seemed to know what he was doing, of course he did, a man of his age. I wondered whether he would believe me if I told him this was only the second time I had slept with a man, probably not.

As I was so inexperienced, I let him do whatever he liked to me and obeyed when he asked me to do things to him. I think it went well, but I didn't know if it had been enough for him to want to see me again. For me it was strange and then everything my body had wanted for so long.

Nick was kind to me afterwards, holding me close

to him in the bed. And now we started to talk. He told me that he was very fond of his wife but that the marriage had gone stale and he no longer wanted to make love to her. I told him that I was fond of my husband. I said we didn't have sex because he had a bad heart, which was sort of true, except we had never had sex, not once in all the years we had been married; but I couldn't say that because I had a daughter and I did not want to have to explain. Perhaps I wouldn't mention Elizabeth.

My eyes had been open for a while now and the old man lying beside me didn't look too bad. He didn't have the muscle tone I had developed from the exercises I did at home, and from my job, but he was not fat and not saggy like Derek.

It's funny, but I couldn't stop thinking about Derek. I had made up my mind before meeting Nick that whatever was going to happen would be completely separate in my mind, and yet here I was, lying in another man's arms and thinking about my husband, who had never properly been that.

I didn't want to talk about Derek to Nick and I didn't want him to talk about his wife. But he did.

Chapter Twenty-Seven

'I'm sorry to say this, but it's her fault I'm doing this. She's let herself go.'

I said nothing and he didn't seem to want me to.

'She's looked after me for thirty years so I don't want to be unkind to her, but she's got her own life really, her job, and there's this man at her office. She spends a lot of time with him, and not just at work. She admits he's her friend, but I'm not sure it's possible for men and women to be just friends.'

'No,' I lied.

'I haven't been in love with her for years, but I've had to think of Sophie – Sophie's our daughter – so I have stuck it out. Sophie lives in London now, the house seems very empty without her. I miss her.'

I wanted to say how much I missed my daughter. Perhaps one of the reasons we were lying in this bed together was because we both missed our daughters. I thought of Elizabeth and how she would be if she knew what I was doing. She loved Derek, her father but not her father. And Derek loved Elizabeth, had done from the start.

We had never mixed much with other people in Ely but anyone we did know thought Derek was Elizabeth's father. She looked like me, which made it easier. Once, when Elizabeth was about seven, we got a taxi home from the station after a day in London, and Baz was the driver. I realised straightaway but pretended I didn't know him so got in and said nothing. When he dropped us off at home, I didn't look at him as I gave him the fare but as I turned towards the house, I heard him say 'Nice to see you again.' That was all. I didn't turn or look at him.

It was more than love, Derek worshipped Elizabeth. When she was a baby, I could put her in his arms as he sat in his chair and if she had been crying, she would stop and the two of them would stare at one another for ages, as if there was nothing more fascinating in the world. I should have been glad, I was glad, but at the same time it made me feel excluded in a way I couldn't make sense of. I've got a photo Derek took of me and Elizabeth when she was a baby and she's looking at me as if I'm a stranger, but perhaps all babies have that look.

It wasn't that long after Elizabeth started school that I realised there wasn't much money. At first Derek had said I could buy anything I wanted for the baby, for myself, so I did. And then I asked him if I could buy presents for Mama and then for my sister. I loved being able to do that because it meant they couldn't criticise me or have a go at me the way they used to.

Then the money sort of dried up. There was a problem with the washing machine and it couldn't be fixed. I thought we'd just get a new one, but Derek didn't mention it and I started washing stuff by hand and that went on and still nothing was said about it.

In the evenings, after I had put Elizabeth to bed, Derek still liked me to come downstairs and sit on the floor beside his chair, rest my head in his lap as he watched television, the programmes I always saw from an angle.

One night he began to stroke my hair, which I liked, and then he told me that we might have to sell the house, get somewhere smaller. Would I mind, he wanted to know. How could I mind? In the core of myself I didn't feel that different from the way I had when I first went to the Rolls' house as the cleaner and all the other things I did, although there had been a washing machine then.

Putting the house up for sale was awful, especially for Derek, who stayed in his chair when people came to look round. He would acknowledge them with a nod and then not look at them again. I would show them the house and through their eyes see all the things that were wrong with it, the big damp patch on my bedroom wall where the guttering outside had broken, the kitchen with its mismatched cupboards and funny old sink, the uneven floor. Sometimes it was if I wasn't there, the people saying to each other how everything would need to be stripped out or wondering whether the roof was as bad as the rest of it. I think some of them didn't realise I was Derek's wife, but why should they?

Nobody wanted to buy the house and I was secretly pleased, I didn't want Mama and my sister to see us have to move somewhere smaller, to see that things were not as they seemed. I knew they would go back to treating me as they had in the past, as a source of shame even if it wasn't my fault, except it would be so clear this time how I had got it all wrong, marrying a man so much older than me and now with no money.

No more treats for any of us.

If nobody was going to buy the house, I started thinking of ways I could get money, so that we could stay. When I went out to buy food, I started looking at the little cards in the window of an employment agency but I didn't have the skills for anything other than the cleaning jobs and the pay was so low I doubted it would help us enough.

One night I was sitting on the floor with my head resting in Derek's lap when I felt him start to shake. I looked up and saw he had tears running down his cheeks. I didn't know what to say. I felt embarrassed for him and at the same time I was revolted by him, his weakness, what he had allowed to happen.

'I'm sorry, my darling,' he said, hoarse with emotion. He sniffed loudly and then blew his nose on a handkerchief I had washed and ironed. That's what I thought, he's blown his revolting snot onto it and now I shall have to wash it tomorrow before it dries too hard.

'I was born in this house, you know. What would my mother say if she knew what's going to happen to it?'

I didn't need to say anything, I knew he would keep on talking, almost as if to himself, as if I wasn't there with my head in his lap, like a child silenced by the sense of bad news pressing in all around us.

'No one is going to buy this house in its present state and I can't afford to do it up. I've had an offer, from a builder. He wants to knock it down and build flats.' He interrupted himself with a horrid gulping sound.

'But what I keep telling myself is that we will be alright all the time we have each other.' His hand, trembling, was stroking my hair again. 'And Betty, of course. Whatever happens, I shall always look after the two of you, you know that, don't you.'

I was thinking in a different direction, how Elizabeth and I might manage by ourselves, but whichever way I thought about this it felt impossible. I didn't have the confidence to go it alone with no money. The supply from Derek might have run dry but surely things would be better when we got the money from the builder. What I didn't know then was that just about all of it would go to pay off debt, and that what was going to happen would make me think back to the time I had spent in this house as the best part of my life.

Chapter Twenty-Eight

Charlotte

It went on for a long time. I would go to the house where I had lived for so many years and throw a brick through the window immediately beyond which I knew Nick would be sitting at his desk. I would confront him and punch him hard in the face. I would go over to the window, grabbing his computer screen on the way and throw it out into the garden. I would sneak into the garage and run a screwdriver the length of his car, making a deep irregular line in the paintwork. I would tell him the awful name the people who worked for him called his 'new partner'.

There were variations on these fantasies, so vivid in my mind's eye, their enactment visualised through a searing hatred I both resented and nurtured.

I had chosen to leave. I could have become Mrs Clark, remained in the marital home. I could have waited for Nick's affair to wither, as surely it would. I could have put up with my husband having sex with another woman – as it turned out, lots of other women. The possibilities were there and yet none felt possible. I had considered Mrs Clark but the difference was that her husband still loved her.

Without fully realising what was happening, I had begun to withdraw from Nick in trivial ways which mattered more than their superficiality. I avoided places where we had been together, I sorted through possessions with associations and packed them off to a charity shop. I developed an aversion to France, which I had loved all my life. I suppose all this was to try and side-step those moments of the dagger through the heart, but you couldn't always dodge them. Hearing about a family gathering which in the past I would have organised. Photographs of someone else on display. Sophie weeping as she told me about it all. These were the sort of things that would not go away, the cruel demon in my head forcing me to think of them over and over.

In the early days I think I came close to throwing the brick, smashing the face. 'But you and Nick were special' a friend said when I told her what had happened.

Towards the end of the summer I was increasingly indulging thoughts about Amit. If I could look at it objectively for even a moment, I knew it was no more than wanting a man to love, to go some way towards filling the jagged hole left by Nick. I think I came close to falling in love with him, although I never imagined him leaving his ailing wife.

The other men I was seeing at that time were like insurance, but they didn't know that, of course they didn't. There again, perhaps they sensed that I was not fully playing the game. Rod was due to visit and I had invited him to come with me to lunch with friends, but early that morning he called me.

'It's not you. It's me,' he said after telling me that 'the spark' had gone. He asked if I wanted him still to come to the lunch. I said no, but the conversation didn't end there. I told him about Amit and he didn't like it. I told him he had been catching up fast. He didn't like that either. That was the end of Rod and I didn't care.

I met the two Jameses that summer. They were both too old. I was viewing men in the same way I might buy a car. Far too much mileage on both the Js. The first was the one who went on and on about how fed up he had become having to take his late wife to and from hospital appointments. I didn't say it must have been worse for her, I'm not like that. I quite liked him, he was straightforward, even if not about his age, although he admitted he had shaved off a few years on his profile. We had arranged to meet again after our initial meeting. I was to contact him; but I left it too long, he found someone else. He sent me a message saying if ever I needed help, he would do what he could, which I found heartening. The second James was a huge man, dishevelled, dirty worn-down shoes. Looking back, I think he might have been more or less homeless and that his main interest was finding somewhere comfortable to live. We met a couple of times (I can't think why). He made a lunge at me the second time, a long, inescapable kiss in full view of everyone sitting outside the pub, and to which I submitted because I didn't want to create a scene. After that he sent me a text saying he didn't think I had the same carnal interest that he obviously had and was bowing out before he got hurt.

He called me one night, said he was locked in a car

compound, a story which sounded too complicated to delve into, but I listened to him, even though he kept getting my name wrong, until it seemed likely he didn't really know who was taking his call.

I found it amusing, this sort of thing, although it might have hurt a little if I had not been waiting for the summer to end and the return of Amit.

He flew down to Stansted for the beginning of term and had asked me to meet him at the airport. He had also asked me to book a nice restaurant for supper.

As I waited for his flight to land, he sent me text messages 'Not long now', 'I'll be with you very soon'. I longed to see him. In the waiting area a man started talking to me and we struck up a conversation. Then he wanted my phone number and I thought, this is amazing, I am far too old. 'I'm meeting my partner,' I told him, and in saying it, I knew it was not true.

When, at last, Amit came through the gates, he looked tired and miserable. I hurried forward and put my arms around him, but the response was not there.

It seems to take such a long time to get away from an airport and as the minutes went by, I could sense rising irascibility wafting from Amit. I think it is only exceptional women who don't feel that a man's ill temper is something to do with them; it's innate to us to put ourselves down as the cause.

I knew something was wrong. The text messages had sounded so eager and yet now that we were together, and after such a long break, it was as if the connection had been lost.

By the time we reached the restaurant, it was nearly

too late to order, but as Amit's was the only Indian face there, I daresay they did not want to turn us away.

As the food came, I was alert to everything Amit said, all of it thick with the type of self-pity that would have found anything in life worthy of its indulgence. He was determinedly miserable, complaining about his college, how he was treated, not appreciated. He said his colleagues were jealous of him. He recounted sleights and other perceived unkindness he must have been brooding over all summer. It was one of those monologues that could have been addressed to a blank wall.

Then he stood up and went outside, without saying why or for how long, without saying anything. I didn't wait long before following him. Something inside me was no longer accepting of unpredictable male behaviour.

'I came out to smoke,' he said, but he was using his phone.

'I'd like a cigarette too.'

He passed me the packet with ill-grace.

We sat down in the dark. I was determined to start a conversation, to get him talking about something other than his perceived troubles. I wanted to listen to him being brainy, I'd never known a professor before. I wanted him to talk in the same way he had when explaining the history of ongoing conflicts, his insights about politics and wars. I wanted to admire him, not pity him. But his mood was irretrievably bleak and introspective.

I was still skimming the surface of desire, perhaps

because I didn't want disappointment. Cigarettes done, we went back to our table inside, the dining room almost as dark as outside. Eating plugged the conversation hole until I heard him mutter 'I am going to make love to you'. Again, it was as if to himself, and I thought it was a given anyway.

Perhaps I was not ready to give up on the idea of Amit, having savoured it all summer, it having kept me afloat and unharmed by Rod's rejection. I wanted to love without commitment, that's what I felt. And this was what had been on offer from Amit from the start. Don't let it end so soon.

Despite such an unpromising evening I duly drove us back to my house and we went to bed. The chemistry was still there, even if I could no longer understand it, and I desperately wanted him to stay the night, to wake up in the morning and find him there. Again, I didn't understand this, only felt it with great intensity. But he wouldn't stay and I knew he never would.

Chapter Twenty-Nine

You hold on to what comes your way until you think you have replaced it. The carapace you have built up around the big crater of despair keeps gathering layers. Don't think about things too much, Nick had said. I didn't, except for the continuing unwanted thoughts about him.

Amit contacted me again not long after the strange night at the restaurant. He sounded more up-beat, suggested we meet, but said it would have to be late because he had a college dinner he had to attend. He would leave early, he said, we could meet at his rooms.

It was a Friday night so I went to the pub as usual for the early part of the evening. Summer had revived itself that year, warm dark evenings, everyone sitting outside. Adam was there and we started one of our conversations about world affairs where we would each take conflicting views because it was more interesting that way. I was waiting for Amit to call with the kind of anticipation which enlivens you to everything. The conversation with Adam was world-beating. So it seemed. But I had drunk too much and suddenly realised it. It was late and still nothing from Amit. Adam casually suggested we go back to his, but it was Amit I wanted.

At last a text came and as I reached for my phone, I saw I had already missed two from him. I called a taxi. Now that I had stopped talking, I had fallen into a muzzy state. I should have told the taxi driver to take me home.

I don't remember going into the college, crossing the courts to reach the building where Amit's rooms were on the top floor. I don't remember climbing the flights of wooden stairs or the place on them where I had paused what seemed like a long time ago, to switch off the call from the folk singer. The remembering starts with pushing open the door and seeing Amit on the sofa, unwelcoming, disgruntled; but I was determinedly upbeat, or perhaps just drunk.

After a moment or two of orienting myself, I saw what was flickering on his computer screen, what he was watching from across the room. It was heavy porn.

Why did I stay?

He hit me with a slipper, on my backside. I remember that. It wasn't vicious, but it was humiliating. Afterwards he told me I had done well to arouse him, like being congratulated on a good essay.

It was just sex. It had always been just sex. I had indulged myself with the notion that it might be more; I had wanted a grand passion to wipe out the one I had lost. Accepting the relationship with Amit for what it was released me from him.

This realisation also told me a lot more about where I was at. The sudden bouts of howling had stopped, the need to love and be loved was no longer paramount, and none of this had anything to do with Amit.

I did not expect to hear from him again. I thought he had been disgusted by me, but I didn't care. It didn't matter. I returned to the dating site with a different perspective. I didn't have to be the one to do all the pleasing.

Chapter Thirty

Simone

'Don't let them know where you live or where you work,' the woman who had told me about Illicit Encounters had said. 'Because when you want to end it and they don't, they might come after you. It's happened, believe me.'

She had shouted this out as we moved towards each other, as we did every morning in the school hall when we were mopping the floor, and even though I knew there was no one else around, I wished she would speak more quietly.

When I met Nick, I couldn't see him as the type who would stalk me but I stuck to the advice I had been given. It was better to be safe than sorry. I liked that, 'better to be safe than sorry', even if what I was doing by meeting Nick was dangerous. It was that, but there was also the possibility of safety.

When we had to leave Mrs Rolls' big old house in Ely, I had stopped feeling safe with Derek. I never said it to him, but I blamed him for letting all the money go. There wasn't even enough to buy something smaller, we had to rent, just like Mama always had. She and my sister were not the same to me after that. They had been jealous of me and at the same time nice to me because I could buy things for them, but when I couldn't do this anymore, they went back to being disrespectful.

I went back to buying things from charity shops. I found a dress once that I thought Mama would like but when I gave it to her, she sniffed it and put it down, giving me a look which made me feel as if I had insulted her.

The rented house was on an old council estate on the edge of town, which meant I had to do a lot of walking, taking and fetching Elizabeth to and from school, going to the shops. Doing all this walking, cleaning the house, doing the washing, cooking, the days went by quickly but it felt as if I wasn't going anywhere. One day, after I had taken Elizabeth to school, I don't know why I did it but I went to look at the old house, except it wasn't there, just a patch of land with a barbed-wire fence round it. I stood and stared at where it had been and screwed my eyes up to try and remember what it had looked like.

That night I told Derek what I had done and how the house had gone. I wish I hadn't. He started to cry. I put my arms round him so I didn't have to look at his face.

'I'm so sorry, my darling Simone. So sorry.' He kept saying it, over and over, until I couldn't stand it. I moved away from him, catching the smell of his old man's breath. I went upstairs to my room, which was the smallest, lay down on the bed and let the usual thoughts come into my head, how I could escape; but there was no escape, there never had been and this was my life.

I must have gone to sleep but something woke me up. I was still fully dressed and lying on top of the bedclothes. I sat up and listened. Then I heard it again, a heavy thud, coming from downstairs. I got up and crept to the door, opened it as quietly as I could. I looked across the hallway to Elizabeth's bedroom door, slightly open, as she liked it, but there was no sound coming out.

Halfway down the stairs there was another thud, this time like something being kicked over. I went back up and into Elizabeth's room. She was asleep and I didn't want to wake her in case she made a noise. I closed her door and sat down on the floor with my back pressed against it.

I listened and listened until the silence was roaring in my head. I stayed like that for a long time, until it started to get light outside. Elizabeth was still asleep but beginning to move about in bed so it wouldn't be much longer before she was awake. I knew I had to go downstairs before that happened but I was frightened to leave her.

When I stood up, I was stiff and my head felt fuzzy from lack of sleep. I opened Elizabeth's door and went out onto the landing. This time I made it all the way downstairs and stopped at the bottom to listen. Nothing. They must have gone. They had probably taken things but the hallway looked the same as it had when I'd gone upstairs the night before. I hesitated outside the living room door and then opened it. I was shaking. Some light was coming through the curtains and then I saw Derek, lying on the floor, the coffee table on its side.

I went over to him, knelt beside him. 'You alright?'

He was breathing and then he opened his eyes. 'You alright?' I said again. He closed his eyes again and I ran to the kitchen where I had left my phone charging the night before.

The ambulance man wanted to know when it had happened.

'I don't know. I was asleep,' I said. Then I told him I couldn't go to the hospital with Derek because my daughter was upstairs and I had to look after her. And then they were gone. I saw a curtain move in the house across the road as I watched them take Derek away. A heart attack, they had said. I didn't feel anything, not until I thought what this would mean, that I would have to nurse him for the rest of his life.

Elizabeth wanted to know why Derek wasn't there and when I told her, she got herself into a state, crying and pushing me away when I tried to comfort her. 'I want to see Daddy. I want to see Daddy,' she screamed at me.

She was too upset to go to school. I took her on the train to Cambridge and then a bus to the hospital. She had stopped crying but now she was very quiet. She wouldn't let me hold her hand.

The hospital was so big, corridors that went on and on, some of them with paintings on the walls. I tried to get Elizabeth to look at them but she wouldn't. 'I want to see Daddy.'

We found Derek. He was sitting up in bed with bits of equipment hanging off him. He looked small. Elizabeth ran to him and before I could stop her she had flung her arms over his chest and buried her face in him.

'My darling. My darling,' Derek said, but he was looking at me. His face was full of gratitude.

I looked away and then tried to pull Elizabeth from him, but she wouldn't move. I didn't know what to do so I sat down on the chair beside the bed and looked around at the other people in the bay, some of them had visitors, others were just mounds under the blankets.

'I'm so very sorry about all this,' Derek was saying to me. 'You don't deserve this, I know that.' From the corner of my eye I could see his hand trying to find mine.

'You must rest and then you will get better,' I said, moving my hand out of reach, wishing we could just go. I hated the smell of the hospital, disinfectant mixed with cabbage. I wanted to get Elizabeth out of there and into fresh air.

I sat still and silent for what seemed like an exceptionally long time, thinking about how soon we could leave without it looking strange. When, at last, Elizabeth and I were outside the ward, a nurse came up to us, the doctor, he said, wanted a word. After a few minutes, a woman with a stethoscope hanging from her neck came up to me, she sat down on the chair next to mine. I think she said something friendly to Elizabeth and then she turned to me: 'Your husband's heart attack is not too serious but he will need to rest and then start taking gentle exercise.' She said some more, about not smoking, and then she lowered her voice and said it would be better if we did not have any strenuous sex. I wanted to laugh then, but I knew better.

Things were not that different from before when Derek came home, except I had decided to get a job, anything to bring in some money. It didn't take long for me to realise that the only possibility was cleaning, something I could do early in the morning before Elizabeth had to go to school, or in the evening after she was in bed. So I found two jobs at either end of the day, one in a school and the other in some offices. At least I knew cleaning was something I could do well.

I didn't tell Mama or my sister about the cleaning jobs, it was bad enough that I no longer lived in the big house. I didn't see them much, I was too busy and too tired.

Derek still liked me to sit beside him before I went to bed, to rest my head in his lap, and now I didn't mind too much, I was so weary, and when he stroked my hair, I liked the feeling.

Chapter Thirty-One

I asked Nick to stroke my hair. He asked me to do a
lot of things to him and when he wanted to know what
I would like, I said the hair stroking. I think it was
then he told me that his wife liked to have her back
scratched, and I don't know why, but my body tensed
up and I pulled away from him.

'What's the matter?' He sounded annoyed. There
was something in his voice I had not heard before.

'Your wife.'

'You're not going to start being silly? We're both
married, for god's sake.'

'Yes.' And in that moment I was thinking about
Derek and how he had never had unkindness in his
voice.

'Look, if I preferred Charlotte to you, we wouldn't
be here in bed together.'

'You still have sex with her, don't you?'

'She'd suspect something if I didn't.'

'I don't want you to have sex with her anymore.'

'You're not jealous?'

'Wouldn't you like me to be?'

'Stop being stupid.'

'Stop talking to me like this, I don't like it.'

'Oh, here we go.'

'What do you mean?'

'Why do women always have to be stupid about
these things?'

'What things?'

It went on like this. I didn't want to stop seeing Nick, my body wanted what he did to it but I couldn't let him be nasty to me. If he thought he could, I knew it would only get worse. I'd never stood up to Mama and my sister but with Nick I had a chance to make things different. I knew how much he wanted me, and that was the difference; I had never felt my family wanted me in any way at all, except when I could buy them things.

'I think we'd better leave it.' His voice had changed again. He had been like a sudden stinging wind and now it had stopped. I would do as he said this time.

I think he might have regretted showing me this other side because he called me the next day and every day after that at the time I had told him was safe. He was nice to me on the phone. He talked about his business a lot and the people who worked for him but I didn't mind, I didn't want to talk about my work, I didn't want him to know what I did. He had asked, at the beginning, and I'd said I helped in a school.

Dating Nick was not easy for me. I couldn't drive and we didn't have a car anyway, so I had to go by train and bus to meet him at the hotels he booked. It meant we did not have a lot of time together.

'This is silly,' he said, but not in his nasty voice. 'I can come and pick you up. Just tell me where.' I wasn't sure about this, suppose someone saw me in his car, not that I knew many people; even so, I was terrified of being found out.

'At least let me meet you at the station.'

I agreed to this and I liked being in his car, it was

big and expensive, I could tell by the leathery smell of the seats and all the dials on the dashboard. But all the time I was in it I kept looking to see if anyone was looking at me.

We went to a hotel where we had been before and as we walked in the receptionist looked at me in a knowing sort of way. I froze, and then I turned and left.

'What's the matter?' He sounded worried, not cross, as he caught me up.

'It didn't feel right. Can we get in the car.'

'What do you mean "didn't feel right"?'

'The receptionist. She recognised me.'

'Does that matter?'

'To me, it does. You can take me back to the station if you like.' I must have said this in a way that bothered him.

'Look, we can go somewhere else.'

'Another place where people will look at me because I'm an Asian with a white man, and all the time we are upstairs, they will know what is happening. It makes me feel cheap.'

He started the car. 'I don't want you to feel like that.' His voice was quiet, as if he was talking to himself as much as to me, as if he was making a decision.

'Where are we going?' I asked after neither of us had spoken for a while.

'I want you to see where I live.'

I didn't reply. I knew he would not take me there unless it was safe, that nobody else would be there. I also realised that this made what was between us serious in a way it had not been before and I couldn't decide if this was what I wanted, and to see what I could not have.

It was not that far. We turned through white gates into a huge driveway with a big house towering above. It was much bigger than Mrs Rolls' old house.

'Don't worry. There's nobody in.'

I followed him up some stone steps and then inside, a flight of stairs to a hallway leading to more stairs, wide and with a heavy wooden bannister which wound up to the next floor.

'I'll show you round.'

This was the largest house I had ever been in. The rooms downstairs had high ceilings and were full of expensive-looking old furniture. There were lots of books lining the walls on one side of what Nick said was the drawing room, and on the other walls there were pictures, some of them quite big.

He took me upstairs and when we went into the main bedroom, his bedroom, he closed the door.

'Nobody is going to see or hear or think it strange.'

He wanted me so badly that we didn't fully undress, and all the time I was listening, in case.

I decided I would never go there again, it was far too risky. The next time we met, we went to a motel, to a horrid room where we had to draw the curtains because the window looked straight out to the car park. This wasn't what I wanted, and if Nick wanted me, he was going to have to do better. This thought seemed to open up something in me I had suppressed all my life. It was the possibility of power.

Lying in bed after we had made love, Nick said he wanted to give me a treat. He wanted to know if there was any way I could be away from home for a night. He said he was going on what he called a 'booze trip', buying wine in France, something he did every few months. He said his wife was going to be away on something called a press trip; he never normally stayed over, but she wouldn't know, it would be our chance to spend a whole night together.

My immediate thought was no, but then it began to seem possible. I could tell Derek I had been invited to go on a shopping trip by a woman I worked with, that we would be going to France on the ferry. I'd have to check my passport had not run out, the one I'd got when Elizabeth had gone on a school trip to Holland and I'd gone as a helper. Elizabeth hadn't wanted me to go, she'd said it would be embarrassing, that none of the other mothers would be going, but I could not imagine letting her leave the country without me. She'd been sullen about it the whole trip, refusing to speak to me.

'Alright.'

Nick hugged and patted me. I felt like a child who had promised to do something brave.

Chapter Thirty-Two

I was better at lying than I thought I would be. The best thing was to say as little as possible and for the things said to be true. I was going on a shopping trip to France. I would be away for one night.

'You deserve a treat,' Derek said, smiling because he wanted something nice for me. 'Betty and I will be fine for one night, although we couldn't be without you for any longer.' What did he mean by this? Did he suspect something?

'It won't cost very much. My friend has got a special deal.' I said.

I got up early and left the house without waking Elizabeth or Derek, I didn't want to think about them. I walked into the town and caught a train to the station where Nick was going to meet me. The thought of spending a whole night with him made me excited but nervous too because it was the next step to I didn't know where.

On the train I picked up a magazine somebody had left on the seat, but I was having to read everything twice and still not taking it in. I watched the countryside pass by, white with frost, and shivered even though the train was warm.

I saw Nick's car as the train drew in and made myself walk rather than run to it. When I got in he leaned over and kissed me and seemed relieved.

'Did you think I wouldn't come?' I don't know why I said this.

'Why would I think that?'

'Anything could have happened.'

'Don't be silly.'

I didn't say any more but the way he spoke made me feel uncomfortable.

The next time he said something he was nice again, and after that we were silent for what felt like a long time.

When his phone rang and it was his wife, I froze, as if she might hear me breathing.

'I thought you'd be at Dover by now,' she said, her voice so close and clear, and I had never wanted to hear it.

'Terrible traffic,' Nick said.

'But you left so early.'

Then the satnav spoke, a woman's voice.

'Who's that? Are you playing away?' She sounded alarmed.

'Of course not. You're paranoid. That's the satnav.'

'I want you to come home tonight.'

'I can't. You know I made an error with the booking. I'll see you tomorrow night.' He ended the call and turned off the phone.

'She knows,' I said. My heart was pounding and I felt a bit sick.

'Of course she doesn't.' He sounded annoyed.

'She sounded worried.'

'You're not going to let this spoil things, are you?'

'It was just hearing her.'

'We're both married. Let's leave it at that.' Then he started to laugh.

'What is it? Why are you laughing?'

'Her thinking the satnav was you.'

'Why is that funny?'

He laughed again. 'It just is.'

'Is this all a joke?'

He didn't answer straight away.

'No, Simone. You know this is no joke. We both know that.' His voice was serious. 'But as I said, we're both married. We knew what we were doing when we went on the dating site but we didn't expect to fall in love.'

Was I in love? I didn't know. I didn't think so, and I didn't want to be told I was, I knew that. I just wanted something for myself, that was all. I tried to think how I could say this without making Nick angry and nasty to me, but there were no words, no words that wouldn't spoil the day and the night ahead. I just wanted now.

Chapter Thirty-Three

On the ferry I felt sick again but I didn't think it was the sea. I kept hearing his wife's voice and wishing I hadn't. Nick wanted to know what was wrong, so I told him I felt sick and he was nice to me about it, saying we should go out on deck to get some fresh air, but it was freezing out there, and it didn't make any difference.

When we got to France, we drove straight to a big shopping complex. In the area where they sold wine, Nick took a long time choosing and then he said he wanted to buy me a present, but first he had to make a call. He said he had to go outside to get a signal and that I was to wait in the warm.

I think he called his wife, but it might have been something to do with his work. When he came back, we went to where cigarettes were sold and he bought two hundred. He had told me before that his wife smoked and how glad he was that I didn't.

We went for a coffee then and when we sat down he put his hand over mine under the table.

He asked me what I would like for a present and I said I would like a ring, one I could wear when we were together. He seemed to like that idea. We found a jewellery shop in the complex and I waited for him to suggest what we should look at as I didn't know how much he wanted to spend.

'You're fingers are so small,' he said, as if making a comparison as I tried on a ring from the tray he had pointed to. All the rings on this tray were silver and something in me seemed to ping at that moment. Silver was second best and today and tonight I was not going to be that. I let him see me look across to where the rings were gold. I could see he was hesitating. Then he nodded to the assistant who quickly brought out the tray of gold rings.

The one I chose had a small opal and tiny diamonds. I loved it. I loved Nick for buying it for me. It made me feel special, and all the feelings I'd been having, the fearful ones, slipped away. Outside the shop I reached up to kiss Nick and I could see he was pleased that I was pleased.

That night we had supper at the hotel where we were staying and I kept feeling the ring on my finger. I think Nick saw this. He smiled. We didn't talk much. We went to bed early and the sex was the best it had ever been, lasting much longer. Nick wanted to keep the light on. He said my body was beautiful. He told me again that we had fallen in love. I did things that night I could never have imagined. Perhaps he was right. Perhaps we had fallen in love. I still didn't know but it was that night I realised I couldn't go back to a life without sex, and the treats that went with it.

On the ferry back to Dover I asked him what he would say to his wife because I was sure she suspected; but he said it wouldn't be a problem, that even if she did suspect, she was sensible enough to pretend she didn't, she had too much to lose.

But she hadn't pretended on that phone call in the car, I thought.

He could see I was worried. 'I want you to know that if we are found out, I will look after you. We can't give each other up, we both know that. If your husband finds out, not that I think he will, unless, of course if you tell him . . .'

'No,' I interrupted.

'But just supposing, and he throws you out. If that happens, I will find somewhere for you to live.'

I didn't know what to say. Nick had just taken away one of the things that most frightened me, being homeless, but he had left out Elizabeth.

'My daughter.'

'I know, but she will be going to college soon, she'll be leaving home.'

'I can't leave her. She's got her exams and I don't want her to be upset.'

'I'm not imposing any time limits. I can wait until you are ready.'

He was making it all sound as if I wanted what he wanted but I had not thought about having to decide. I wanted to be safe and I was with Derek, even if there wasn't much money. I didn't think I would ever feel really safe with Nick.

Chapter Thirty-Four

It was late when I got home. I kissed Elizabeth but she didn't kiss me back and I thought maybe she was cross with me for going on a shopping trip without her. Derek wanted to know if I'd had a good time and when I said yes, he said he was glad. I suppose I had been avoiding looking at him but then I did and I could see he was unwell.

I went closer to where he was sitting. I could smell the stale tobacco smoke on him; it was strange how I didn't normally notice it but two days away and it seemed so strong.

'Are you okay?'

He smiled at me, that pathetic smile of his. 'I'm alright, my darling, just a bit tired.'

'I'll make some coffee for you.' I wanted an excuse to leave the room. As I went towards the door he said: 'Betty and I missed you.'

I wondered what to say about the trip, especially as I had bought nothing and couldn't show off what had been bought for me, apart from some chocolates. I had to say something or it would seem suspicious. While I made coffee, I tried to work out what I could say; as little as possible would be best or I might trip myself up in a lie.

When I took the coffee to Derek, I sat down on the floor beside him, just as I always did, and that made it easier as I could rest my head in his lap and not have to look at him.

'Tell me about it all.'

'I felt sick on the ferry.'

'I hope your friend looked after you.'

'She did. She was nice.'

'You could invite her to come here. It worries me, you know, that you never have any friends round.'

'I don't want to.'

'Is it the house? I know it's not what we'd like.'

'No, it's not the house.'

'I hope you bought something nice for yourself.'

'We haven't got any money.' I shouldn't have said that. I felt Derek's knees shift a little. He sighed and began to stroke my hair.

Nick had wanted to meet as usual the following week, but I had said I couldn't make it, I felt I needed some time to get back into the way my real life was. I thought about what he had said, about finding me somewhere to live if Derek found out, but I couldn't rely on him always wanting me. I had to make sure I didn't get found out. Perhaps it was all getting too dangerous.

And then it happened. Late one night, a text: 'She knows. What do you want to do?'

I didn't reply straightaway but then I began to worry that he might call me.

'I don't want my name mentioned,' I texted. It was all I could think to say. I lay in bed, my heart thumping so hard because I didn't know what would happen next. I had to keep safe. All the worrying thoughts I'd been pushing away filled my head now. What his wife might do, whether she would find me. What would happen when Derek found out? He had never said an angry word to me but nothing like this had ever happened before. He might throw me out, he might. And Elizabeth, I would lose Elizabeth. And where would I go? Nick had said he would find somewhere for me but I don't think I believed he really would. The only possibility was to go back to Mama, but the humiliation would be too much.

I was too restless to stay in bed, to even stay in my room. I got up and went downstairs. I thought maybe Derek would have gone to bed by now but I could hear the television. I pushed open the door and went over to him, kneeling down and putting my head in his lap as I always did and in that moment never wanting to be anywhere else.

'Couldn't sleep, darling?' He had begun to stroke my hair and after a little while I felt calmer. I reached up and put my arms round him, burying my face in his chest. If only I could tell him and it wouldn't matter.

When at last I went upstairs again, there was another text from Nick.

'I promise I won't betray you but I have to know what you want to do.'

It wasn't that easy. He must know. I didn't want to give him up but I couldn't risk everything. I couldn't risk Elizabeth.

Then my phone rang. I answered quickly, afraid of the ring tone.

'I'm sorry to call you.' His voice sounded strained. 'I must know what you want to do.'

I put my head under the bedclothes, the phone

pressed hard against my ear as if this would hold back the sound.

'I don't know. I haven't thought about it,' I said very quietly.

'You must have.' Then: 'I'm sorry, I don't want to put pressure on you.' You do, I thought. You do.

'Charlotte is being very calm about it, at the moment, anyway. I've told her I won't give you up.'

'She might find me.'

'I don't think she will.'

'How do you know that?'

'You'll have to trust me.'

'This is serious,' I said.

'So what do you want to do?'

Everything had changed but I wanted it all to be as if it hadn't, so I said: 'I want to go on dating.'

After the call was over I wondered whether I could, but two days later I met him as we had arranged. He was waiting at the station and when I first saw him, there was a moment when he seemed like a stranger, an old man in a big expensive car.

When I got in, he reached his arm across to pat my hand, as if I had done the right thing.

Chapter Thirty-Five

'It must be difficult for you,' I said.

'You could say that.' He sounded angry, as if it was all my fault.

'I'm sorry.'

'She says she's leaving. She says six months, to think things over, but I don't think she'll come back.'

'Can't you stop her?'

He laughed, just a little.

'If I agreed to give you up.'

I didn't know what to say.

'She's being too hasty. I've said we can go on living together, as friends. I don't think she likes sex, so that should suit her.' He was speaking as if to himself. 'I certainly don't want to sleep with her any more. And she's being selfish. It's going to upset Sophie, her leaving. I'd say she's got everything the way she wants it now, so why leave?'

'I don't think you want to lose her,' I said quietly.

'And you don't want to lose your husband and your daughter.' He said this nastily, as if I was being selfish too.

I didn't like the way he was being and when we went into the motel room, I thought about telling him we shouldn't see each other anymore, but I was frightened about how he might behave towards me.

When we were in bed, his mood seemed to change and he was nice to me.

'All this was bound to happen, you know. It's not

really your fault,' he said after the sex.

I didn't say anything.

'I've found her boring for a long time. I wouldn't have looked elsewhere otherwise.'

Each time we met after his wife had found out, I became more scared. I thought she might get a private detective to find me, and the easiest way was to have Nick followed.

Nick must have noticed how nervous I was and when I told him what I had been thinking, he said I mustn't worry, that he didn't think his wife would do anything like that, and, besides, she hadn't got the money to pay somebody to find me. I didn't really understand this. Nick obviously had money, so why didn't his wife?

Then Derek had another heart attack. Elizabeth called me while I was in bed with Nick.

'Where are you?' she screamed, I could hear she was crying.

'I'll take you to the hospital,' Nick said.

'No. We'll be seen.'

'Don't be silly. Who is going to see us if I drive you there and drop you off. You can say the friend you were with gave you a lift. That's what you always say, isn't it? That you are out with a friend?' He sounded impatient with me, as if I had spoiled our time together.

He was nice again in the car, telling me not to worry too much. It was as if he had thought of something that pleased him, but I was thinking about Elizabeth, the way she had sounded on the phone.

When I found her, she was sitting alone. She seemed relieved to see me but there was something else, as if she wanted to hold back from me, as if I had let her down. I didn't know what to do so I took the seat beside her and asked what was happening.

'They're looking after him. They said they're looking after him.' There was an awful bleakness in her voice. Then she said: 'I found him. He was lying on the floor. I thought he was ...' Her voice trailed off, she couldn't bear to say it. In that moment I wondered whether she would be as upset if she had found me on the floor, which was an awful thought to have.

When Derek came home, I did my best to be a good nurse. I didn't leave the house unless Elizabeth was there and then only to get the shopping and to do my cleaning work. I told Nick I couldn't see him for a while, but I was thinking it had to be over. I wouldn't let myself think about him during the day but at night, when I was at last in bed, I couldn't help it. I realised that I didn't really like him but I still wanted him.

Chapter Thirty-Six

Nick

It wasn't my intention to leave C. I didn't fancy her anymore but the prospect of what might happen if we parted was not on my agenda. I would have been quite happy to carry on as I had over the past year, seeing Simone once a week; I had not gone on the dating site with the idea of finding a new partner.

As far as C was concerned, I managed to grit my teeth and have sex with her, I didn't want to give her a reason to suspect I was going elsewhere. I'd had flings in the past and if she had guessed, she never said anything, although I don't think it crossed her mind. The point about the earlier affairs was that they made me want C more. I can't explain this. The point about Simone was quite different.

When I first saw her, at the hotel, I knew I had to have sex with her. She wasn't a great looker, I think it was more that she was mysterious, and exotic, I'd never had an Asian woman. She was reticent at first but when we went to bed, she was a delight and I could hardly believe my luck at my age. I told C, when it all came out, that I just wanted to see what was out there, before it was too late, and this was the truth. These things don't need to be complicated.

Right up to the last minute, I tried to avoid telling C, but when it became clear that Sophie had said something, I knew it was crunch time.

I think my effort to sell C the Mrs Clark scenario was half-hearted, looking back. I still had feelings for her but they faded fast after she left me. I thought she had made a mistake, the house was big enough for us to go on sharing and at the same time live independent lives. Lots of people did that.

She'd asked me how I would feel if she slept with someone else, and I thought it was only kind to say I wouldn't like it; to tell her to go ahead would have been cruel, especially as I thought it unlikely she would find anyone, the state she was in. So it was a bit of surprise when she stayed out all night the same week I told her. I felt oddly jealous, but that would fade, I was sure of that.

She didn't say she had slept with someone but all the signs were there and I had a good idea who it was.

She came breezing into the house, it was early. I was already up and dressed, sitting at the dining room table reading the paper. She made breakfast for us, although she didn't eat any herself. She had a false brightness about her. I knew very well that the only reason she had done what she had was revenge, and that was disconcerting, because she had never been a vengeful woman.

I'd got up early because I was going to collect a new car, and it was this that gave me the first indication that she was going to be difficult. I needed her to sign something so that I could get the car on the company and I thought she was on the point of doing so when she hesitated and said she couldn't.

We both went out that day. I got the car, I bloody

well deserved it. She saw it when she came home and immediately challenged me, accused me of forging her signature. I had it down to a fine tee.

If all this makes me sound dishonest, well, so be it. I had forged her signature many times on documents it was in her own interest not to see, she would only have worried. When you are in business, you must cut corners in some departments if you are going to survive. You'd be a fool not to.

I'd had one business fail on me and I wasn't going to let it happen again. I warned C, on the day she left, that if she tried to back me into a corner as far as the business was concerned, she knew what I would do. She had never played any part in the business so she didn't deserve anything, and she wouldn't get it.

When she said she wanted to go away for six months, I had told her if she did, I thought it unlikely she would come back. I knew there was only one way she wouldn't go and that was for me to say I'd stop seeing Simone. I could have pretended. The truth is I couldn't be bothered. I'd had it with C. It was her choice.

Living alone, something I'd never done before, was not what I would have chosen. I had missed Sophie a great deal when she left home and missed her even more after C left me on my own. I wanted to see Sophie but I knew she was angry and upset, so I confined myself to texts. She didn't always answer them, in fact not very often, and this began to annoy me. I was still sending her a monthly allowance and threatening to stop this seemed the only way to get her to be more reasonable. It worked.

I didn't intend to say anything against C to Sophie, that would not have been wise, but I hoped that in time she would understand why I had done what I had. Hoped, but I could not plan my life around it. Increasingly, I realised that my future was with Simone, that I had to have her. Carys had said that you need different people for the different stages of your life, and she was right.

When C and I were still meeting, after she had left, I found I could talk to her more honestly than I had in years. We were in a pub one night – our meetings were always in pubs – talking about the only topic C wanted to discuss at this time. I told her that Simone would not leave her husband, that he'd had a second heart attack, and how she did not want to upset her daughter and certainly wouldn't leave until she'd finished her education.

'And then? What will you do then? Wait for her husband to die?'

I said yes.

'That's awful.'

'Is it?'

Another time we met I told her about this idea I'd had, that Simone and her husband and daughter could all come and live with me. To be fair to C, she had always been prepared to listen to my ideas, but perhaps I had gone too far with this one. Any sort of ongoing friendship with her, if only for the sake of expediency, more or less disappeared after that.

This was a difficult time for me. C had gone,

Sophie was no more than polite, and it was looking increasingly unlikely Simone would leave her husband. I thought about going back to the dating site, but the only woman I wanted right now was Simone, quiet and mysterious, sexy as hell, and seemingly unobtainable.

I had always been good at selling, listening was the trick, but Simone didn't say a lot, so I'd have to come up with something else. I had thought it was mainly concern about her daughter that prevented her from leaving and coming to live with me, but I don't think it was entirely that; her daughter would come round to the idea, just as Sophie, in time, would accept what had happened. That's when I made the connection, money. Simone wanted security, she also liked things. I had bought her more stuff, clothes mainly. Going to shops with her and watching her try things on, it reminded me of when C and I were first together and I had chosen a new wardrobe for her. Shopping made Simone more animated. At other times she held herself back from me, as if she was enacting a clichéd way of behaviour that was supposed to maintain my interest. I'd find this irritating sometimes and then we'd have sex and any sense of irritation would dissipate.

One of the irritations was her refusal to come to the house; we didn't need to go to hotels any more but she had this fixed idea that C might suddenly turn up. I pointed out that the locks had been changed but this didn't make any difference.

We were in a motel room one afternoon when a cleaner let himself in. Simone immediately slid down the bedclothes to hide and after the door had been closed again, she went cold on me.

'We'd be much better off at the house,' I said.

She remained silent.

'I'm not prepared to do this anymore.' I meant motels but Simone misunderstood.

'You want to end it?'

'Of course not. Don't be so ridiculous.'

'Don't speak to me like that.'

'Like what?'

'You know like what.'

'You sound just like Charlotte.'

'Did you speak to her like that?'

'I don't know what you are talking about.'

'And I don't know why you are like this sometimes. It makes me sad. When we meet like this, it should be a good time, for both of us. Otherwise, what's the point?'

In that moment I could feel her slipping from me and I wasn't prepared to let that happen. If we were going to stop seeing one another, I was going to be the one to put an end to it.

Chapter Thirty-Seven

It was soon after this unsatisfactory meeting I saw C again. We had not been in contact for several months, apart from her panicking about her solicitor's bills, which I had paid. Don't ask me why, there was every reason not to, it was like giving bullets to the enemy. She wanted to come to the house to collect some more of her stuff. She had to ring the bell because I really had changed the locks, those first few weeks after she left I didn't want her creeping in when I wasn't there and looking through files, taking things without my knowledge. I was sure she had been in before the new locks, I told Sophie this in a text, but she said her mother had not been near the house. Even so, I noticed that the toast tongs had gone from the kitchen drawer and I knew I'd used them since she'd left.

When I went to the door to let C in, it was quite a shock, she had lost a lot of weight. She greeted me in a friendly way, which was another surprise, I'd expected her to be taciturn at best. I let her go upstairs by herself and returned to my study, which was the only place I didn't want her poking about.

After a while I heard her coming down the stairs, so I went out into the hallway. I could hardly believe how much she had changed, she was wearing a tight-fitting summer dress, her hair was up, she looked good.

Before I had given it a second thought, I suggested we could go to the place down the road and have a bit of lunch. I was surprised again when she agreed. An odd thing happened as we left the house, the cat came too and followed us down the street, something it had never done before. We had to shoo it back and I think both of us had the same thought, that the cat saw us as together again.

It was a sunny day, so we sat outside the wine bar. As the food came, someone who we vaguely knew walked past and nodded to us. Thankfully, he didn't stop to speak. I can't remember what C and I chatted about to start with, only that she told me she found herself in the same situation I was in, that she was seeing someone who was married and that he too was Asian. I'm not sure how I felt about this but I know it wasn't jealousy, I'm certain of that.

C hardly touched her food, perhaps she was making a point. She sipped her wine and talked about nothing in particular, I can't remember, only that I interrupted her with a comment about a car going past.

'I hate the way you do that,' she said.

'Do what?'

'You know.'

I thought it better to let it go. I went inside to pay the bill and when I came out she wasn't there. I assumed she had gone back up to the house. It turned out she had gone to the loo. This was a bit awkward as I didn't want her to think I had deliberately left without her, not now it seemed she was going to be reasonable.

I sent her a text later that afternoon telling her how well she had done, the complete reinvention of herself. She didn't reply. She could at least have said thank you.

That meeting made me feel uneasy in a way I had not expected. It occurred to me that C had lost weight, got a new wardrobe, changed her hair in a bid to get us back together again, and the problem was I wouldn't have minded although I would not give up Simone, not until I was ready. Having this thought made me realise that I was already thinking about ending the affair; if Simone was not going to leave her husband, I could not envisage continuing with the way it was. I suppose there had been an added frisson when C didn't know.

I didn't normally stop for lunch so there was work to catch up on when I got home and I didn't think about C or Simone until later when I sent the text. I worked on until nine or so, looked at my phone once or twice to see if C had replied. No doubt she wanted to keep me waiting.

There were no messages from anyone that night. I watched television while I ate a ready meal I had heated and tried not to think about C and her Asian, Simone and her husband. I felt something like dislike for all of them, couldn't concentrate on the news properly, wondered where the cat was hiding.

Chapter Thirty-Eight

What a cow. I'd warned her not to back me into a corner but she had chosen to go for me. For some months I had thought she'd seen sense, her brother had been deployed to try and work out a deal without any further involvement from solicitors. Charles, who was an accountant, had gone through the books and in his polite way had said they were in a mess. God, I knew that, but I was not prepared to spend a fortune on professionals of any kind, bloody leeches. I hate them, the way they make their grubby fortunes out of other people's businesses and misery.

So I let Charles carry on, and some of the stuff he told me was quite useful. He knew his stuff, but what he didn't understand was how you had to cut corners. I sensed his disapproval when the absence of such corners became apparent.

Towards the end of the summer, he came up with a deal which he brought to me rather than email, saying he wanted to go through it face-to-face. It would have been better by email.

In brief, the deal gave C a huge sum of money, forty per cent of the company, which Charles had valued from the accounts after he'd finally got them into what he considered a satisfactory state. To achieve this, there was a deadline for the company to be sold.

I had every right to be angry. In a less than polite way, I told Charles where he could stuff his deal. I could see that he was angry too, but he chose to leave rather than argue.

Then C's solicitor started writing to me again, and this time C needn't think I was going to foot the bill. Against my better judgement, I arranged to have a one-off meeting with a solicitor. He had a practice in the High Street and I recognised his face. He was fat and friendly, two aspects I did not find particularly appealing. I showed him the deal Charles had come up with, expecting him to see quickly how ludicrous it was.

After he'd read through it, he slapped it on the desk and said: 'You need to go back to your brother-in-law and accept the offer. I couldn't get you a deal as good as this.'

My first thought was 'lazy bastard, you don't want the work', and he must have seen that I wasn't pleased.

'In a marriage as long as this one, any court would rule fifty/fifty and I have known cases where it has gone sixty/forty in the wife's favour, especially if there have been children and her earning capacity is not as good as yours.'

What I had not wanted to hear was beginning to sink in. I thought about it as I went home; I could agree to the deal and even though it contained a time limit for selling the business, I could easily drag that out for years, until I was ready to sell.

I composed a careful email to Charles, saying I would accept what he proposed. I tried to make it sound as if I was being magnanimous. A couple of days later Charles replied saying he had spoken to C and the deal was no longer on the table. She also wanted the house to go on the market.

Self-pity is nauseating but I did feel bad. I was the one who had put all the effort into the business and now it looked as if I could lose it, and the house, which didn't leave me with much. I was still seeing Simone most weeks and being with her gave me an hour or two of relief from it all; but gradually I realised that I was thinking about what I could do, even when we were making love. I was also feeling increasingly resentful towards Simone's husband, too ill for her to leave. I can't even say I felt sorry for him, how can you have those sorts of feelings for someone you have never met? I thought of him as standing in the way of my future with Simone.

She was the only person I could talk to without having to be careful what I said. I didn't want Carys or any of the people who worked in the company to start getting jittery about what might happen.

I'd kept myself to myself for some time at this point and it seemed like a good idea to join Carys and the others for the Friday night drinks they had at the place where I'd taken C for lunch, which was the last time we'd had any direct contact.

They'd all had a few by the time I arrived, Carys in particular. She became over-familiar when she was drunk and as soon as I appeared, she came over and started draping herself round me. I knew I could have had her a long time ago but I had made that rule, not to tread there, never again with staff. It put me at a disadvantage.

I eased Carys off me, saying I was going to the bar

to get a round of drinks for everyone.

'I'll come and help you,' Carys said, her speech a little slurred.

At the bar she leaned in close to me as we waited for service.

'You must be so lonely,' she said in a loud whisper.

I was about to refute this when it occurred to me that it would do no harm for her to think I was the wronged party; after all, C had left me, and nobody knew about Simone. I needed to keep the staff on side, it was imperative there was no suggestion of anything happening to the company.

'The customer is king.' You couldn't mistake that voice. I glanced down the bar and saw Barry, the first time in years. Lost all his hair, gained a huge amount of weight. I thought I might catch his eye, it was so long ago when I'd fired him – for his own good – but he had turned away, probably didn't see me.

I ordered the drinks and Carys and I squeezed through the throng with a tray, back to where the others were sitting, half a dozen of them, all constantly worried about their jobs because I liked to keep them thinking they were not up to it. If that sounds harsh, it's not. Running a business is about keeping everybody on their toes, something Barry had failed to grasp, always too friendly with the staff.

After I'd fired him, the company had collapsed, even though I'd thought at the time his going might save it. Not long after, he bought the remnants of the business from the receiver. I thought he was an idiot. As far as I knew, the company was still going; someone

I knew had said it was doing well, but I doubted it.

That night, when I got home, the house felt cold and empty, I'd never noticed this so much before. C had taken a lot of stuff, the best bits, of course. I found myself thinking about her. She was such a fool. She could have stayed, she should have stayed, kept the family home together. She wasn't interested in sex anymore. My suggestion that we live together as friends would have been the best solution. And then she had to go and say all that stuff about me on bloody Facebook.

I made myself a coffee and sat down in front of the television to watch Newsnight but I couldn't concentrate. I was determined to hold on to the business and the house, it was just a question of how best to achieve this.

Chapter Thirty-Nine

Charlotte

Being badly hurt is not something you allow to happened a second time, not when it comes to men. I had felt passionate about Amit, was prepared to be 'the other woman' in his life, had worked out that it rather suited me to have this sort of relationship. I had nourished the idea of him like a treat and not thought much beyond this. I felt no guilt that he was married, accepted what he had said about his wife being sick. It never occurred to me that he would leave her, and because she was so far away, it seemed very unlikely she would find out, or perhaps she knew and didn't care. Amit had told me she had a separate flat in the family home. I believed him.

After the slipper episode I had not expected to hear from him again. Weeks went by and my social life – something I had not really had for years – was jam-packed. Most of it revolved around the pub and the friends I had made there, but I was still looking on the dating site, caught up in it like playing a one-armed bandit.

I don't think I spent a night in during this time; going out had, from the start, been my way of escaping the misery of thinking about Nick, even if there had been moments when I'd been unable to stifle sobbing in public. It would come without warning, and I wouldn't even feel embarrassed or ashamed, entitled to my unbearable sorrow.

This lessened, it had to. There had been the moments when I thought of my life as over but I wasn't depressed. As I've said, I had suffered from this in the past, so I knew the difference between it and plain sadness. At the same time there was this huge and unexpected adrenalin, driving me on to make a new life for myself, and that was exciting.

I didn't feel the same about the battle now raging with Nick, which made the adrenalin doubly necessary. He had warned me not to back him into a corner and I knew this would be how he felt now and that to him this would justify all sorts of tricks to try and cheat me out of my share of the business and the house.

Before handing things over to the solicitor, my brother had spotted some anomalies in the accounts which suggested Nick was moving money offshore. My solicitor said the only thing we could do was impose a freezing order.

This hadn't been in place very long before I found out that he was attempting to sell a block of flats the company had bought as an investment. The solicitor viewed this as Nick raising enough money to pay me off while he conveniently ignored the fact that half the block belonged to me.

The freezing order had caused friction between Nick and my solicitor. This was not surprising but Nick had turned nasty on her, firing off misogynistic personal insults. She had a thick skin but she really didn't like him now. She was out to get him.

'He could go to prison for this,' she told me.

How did I feel about this? Did I want him punished in this way? The answer was no, but only because of Sophie.

I didn't see Sophie as much as I would have liked. She was busy in London but from time to time I was able to have a word with her boyfriend to find out how she was. He was a godsend, that man, sure and steady, and clever, which was exactly what Sophie needed. I would have worried a lot more if he hadn't been there.

He said Sophie was upset but coping, but she had lots of little ailments which he thought were symptomatic. It made me feel wretched to think that Nick was still causing her grief. I knew he loved her, but his kind of love was conditional and controlling. Make her respond to him, make her cry.

The solicitor said there was no choice but to take Nick to court for breaching the order. I followed her advice.

The case was heard in London, a barrister employed. It was going to cost at least £10,000. This frightened me. I had hardly any money, while Nick was sitting on millions in cash and assets.

On the day of the hearing I had to get up early to catch the London train and reach the family court. My bag was searched on the way in, a tiny pair of scissors confiscated. Did they think I might leap up and stab him? Perhaps it had been known. All that blood to clear up.

Think straight. Think straight.

I dreaded the thought of seeing him, the possibility of something stirring in me that would be so unwanted at this juncture.

My solicitor had arrived and took me to a small room along a corridor of small rooms created, I was to discover, for horse-trading. The barrister came in, a fat man full of bluster and excitement. He told us he had just found out his offer on a skiing chalet in one of the most exclusive resorts in the Alps had been accepted. What did this say about him? He was a show-off. Perhaps this was good. My solicitor was smiling inscrutably.

We went through what was hoped to be achieved from the hearing, which was to stop Nick in his tracks and get him to pay my legal costs. This was where the trading began, with fatty coming and going between our small room and another along the corridor where Nick and his brief (at the last minute he'd got one) were ensconced.

The first time he returned, the barrister said Nick was prepared to pay half my costs. I think I came to life at this point, the full realisation that I had to fight him, forget about dread, pursue what I knew was right, my right. I said it had to be the whole lot as none of this had been caused by me.

There were more comings and goings, it was like a bedroom farce. My solicitor and I waited. I can't remember what we talked about. I was thinking all the time whether I wanted to see Nick. I no longer knew how I felt about him. Distance had certainly brought disenchantment, but I just didn't know what I would feel in the courtroom, with me on one side and him on the other after more than thirty years of always being on his side when he'd been up against it.

Our case was called and we left the little room to walk down the corridor to the courtroom. There were men ahead of us and I realised after a moment of non-recognition that one of them was Nick. Of course, I could see only his back, but that included the nape of his neck, a sight which in the past had prompted desire.

Inside the courtroom we were directed to either side, some distance between us. I didn't look at him, kept my gaze firmly ahead to where the judge was sitting. Both barristers spoke, but not for long; the judge had the papers from their discussion.

When the judge started speaking, it was as if none of this had anything to do with me, it was about defying the court. Nick was reprimanded for his behaviour, breaking the freezing order. The judge ordered him to pay all my costs.

I thought he would be angry but on the way out I glanced at him and there was a smirk on his face, as if he thought he had won. It stayed with me, that smirk. What would be his next move? Dread returned. I forgot to retrieve the scissors.

Chapter Forty

Now there was another dread, losing my new home, the thought of having to move again. I had taken the terraced cottage for a year but after six months the housing market went mad and I needed to buy before it went any higher or I wouldn't be able to buy at all. The only way I could become a homeowner again was to sell the house in France as quickly as possible and to get a loan, I was too old for a mortgage.

I had become friendly with the woman who had been Laura's lodger. She had moved across the road, renting a small room at the back of the house where she not only slept but worked, a commute of two steps, from bed to computer. Not so many years ago Delia had lived in a large old house in France with her husband and children, dogs and cats. The marriage had gone wrong in much the same way as mine, Delia had left and bought another house nearby while her daughter finished school, her son was at university in England. Soon after buying the new house, the property market in France bombed and Delia fell into negative equity. A few years on and she was back in Britain, penniless and with a huge debt. She couldn't even afford to rent a house, only a room in someone else's. It all seemed so unfair, but fairness, I was now discovering for myself, was never a given. Nick had been ordered to pay my costs in court but he still held all the cards as far as I could see. Without money to hand, I was powerless to fight.

My solicitor knew this and soon after the court hearing she sent me information about taking a loan to meet my legal bills. The terms were extremely onerous because the risk was considered high, with no ready collateral.

I didn't know what to do. My brother, who I would have turned to for advice, was now seriously ill and I didn't want to bother him or Mary. My solicitor could not advise me on this one. My daughters would not know and I didn't want to worry them. There was no one I could ask who would know any more about it than I did. All I could think was 'when in doubt, do naught'.

But there was still the matter of the house. I wanted to stay where I was, but if the market carried on the way it was going, I would not be able to afford to buy it, even if, and this seemed unlikely at this stage, a financial settlement was agreed with Nick. I knew I would get something eventually, but timing was the issue, just as it had been for Delia.

Thoughts of Amit had faded. I was over that initial urgency to love and be loved, to replace what I had lost. Then, after weeks of silence I received a text from him. He wanted us to meet for supper but I knew he meant more than this. I suppose I wanted to find out if the chemistry would be there again when I saw him. I agreed to a meeting.

I walked into town. It was a pleasant evening, the sun still shining. We had arranged to meet outside the restaurant but I couldn't see him in the street. I walked past, strolled up to the bridge over the river, stopped and gazed at the line of punts by the quayside and realised I was enjoying my surroundings, that I was in the moment.

After a minute or two I strolled back towards the restaurant and then I saw him, sitting on a low wall on the other side of the road. I had glanced at him the first time I had passed and not recognised him.

During supper he poured out his woes to me, the same old perceived jealousies and sleights of his academic colleagues, the stuff I had listened to in the past and not properly dissected as revealing a man whose obsession with himself would never be overcome. I was bored by him, this was the disappointing truth.

Even so, I duly went back to his rooms and we had sex. As soon as it was over, I got out of bed and began to dress. He had gone to the bathroom and when he came back he looked at me in surprise.

'You're dressed. Are you going?'

How things turn about. I thought of the time when I had longed for him to stay the night with me and he wouldn't.

The texts kept coming, albeit infrequently. I missed the thrill I had felt in the past at receiving them.

What occupied my mind now was my housing situation. I had told Laura that I wanted to buy her house and she had decided to put it on the market to see how much she could get for it. The agent came round and told me he was going to advise what he called 'open house' which would mean my home being exposed to anyone who fancied a look. The market was so crazy now that asking prices were largely irrelevant, jumping up £10,000 by the week. Unfortunately, the same was not the case in France.

Then it seemed as if things might be falling into place. Charles, still trying to help even though he was ill, somehow managed to persuade Nick to lend me a portion of what was mine and a buyer materialised for the French house. This all happened in a matter of days and put me in a position to make a firm offer to Laura. The relief was massive, but I should have known better.

I was at work when the agent phoned. He wanted to let me know that a For Sale sign had been put up and a date fixed for the 'open house'.

Maddened, possibly insane, I drove back to the house and immediately spotted the signs, nailed to the wall upstairs, creating a protruding triangle. As I got out of the car, a man from across the road was coming out of his house; I shouted to him, asked if he had a ladder so that I could take down the sign. He looked at me with the shrinking gaze of someone faced with the antics of a mad person. He did have a ladder, he said, but it was in the loft and he had to get to work. He was gone.

I dashed into the house and upstairs to examine how the sign had been attached, huge screws. I hurtled back down the stairs and rummaged in a kitchen drawer to find anything that might loosen them. I found a large pair of scissors, back upstairs, out of the window and onto the ledge.

If I had come to my senses at that moment, I think I would have fallen, but I was driven on by the task in hand, wrenching at the screws until suddenly the sign collapsed into the front garden. I felt triumphant as if at last power had been restored to me.

On the way out I threw the sign into the dustbin and went back to work.

That evening I went for a drink with Tony and told him about my madness, now subsiding with the knowledge that I had yet to convince Laura to sell me her house. Tony listened and thought and came up with an idea. The price I had offered Laura was going to be my absolute maximum but at the bottom of the garden there was a shed which had been turned into a studio flat. It was let to a girl who had been there for a while, I rarely saw her, the shed had its own access.

'Offer Laura the rent on the shed for the rest of the year,' Tony said.

The psychology worked. The sum involved was tiny compared with what I would be paying for the house, but the idea appealed to Laura and she agreed to take the house off the market and sell to me.

I didn't know what I would do without Tony, not just for his clever way of seeing things but for his willingness to involve himself in problems that were not his. He was steadfast. He was my friend.

But he was not my lover and never would be. Nick knew this but when faced with my petition for divorce, citing his affair with Simone, he decided to hit back, citing Tony.

Chapter Forty-One

Simone

I was so tired. Getting up so early to go to my cleaning job, then all day fetching things for Derek who hardly moved from his chair, all the other things I had to do in the house and then more cleaning work in the evening. I ached all over. My hands were stiff and painful. I didn't know how long I could carry on like this. The only thing I still did for myself was seeing Nick, and I wondered how much longer that could go on. One day, when we were in bed, I fell asleep. When I woke I said I was sorry, he didn't pay for a hotel room for me to go to sleep. Instead of being cross, he took me in his arms and told me he wanted to look after me. He said he wanted me to have an easy life, that it really was time I left Derek and went to live with him.

'But what if you get tired of me?' I heard myself say.

'That's always a risk.' He paused, kissed the top of my head. 'But I can't imagine it happening. I know you're worried about being insecure. I have decided to give you half my house and make you the sole beneficiary of my will, so you will always have security, no matter what happens.'

I could hardly take this in.

'By sole beneficiary I mean you will get everything I have when I die. You will never have to worry about money again. You will not have to work, and when your daughter accepts what you have done – which she will in time – she can come to us whenever she likes.'

I shifted in his arms so that I could see his face, and for just a moment I saw that he was afraid. He had nothing more to offer.

At home, that night I felt different. Nick had told me in the past that he wanted me but I had not realised how much. I had always thought he would grow tired of me, just as he had of his wife and the one before her. He had said how he had become bored and discontented with them and I didn't think so much of myself to believe the same would not happen to me. I always made myself look as good as I could for our dates but I was worried about my tiredness showing and that he would get fed up. I had also thought his wife might go back to him and accept that he was still seeing me. I didn't know what sort of person she was, Nick did not say much about her; I didn't expect him to or want to hear. I preferred not to think about her.

But I couldn't stop thinking about Elizabeth and how she would feel if I left. For me, the worst thought was that she wouldn't care, and this was the possibility I could not face.

The next time I saw Nick he wanted to know if I had thought about what he'd said. I had, I told him, but couldn't leave until Elizabeth had completed her education. He accepted this because I had said 'until'; I saw the look on his face, he thought he had me.

In the evenings at home I still sat on the floor by

Derek and put my head in his lap. I continued doing this because I didn't want him to suspect me, I had to keep things the same. Sometimes Elizabeth was there too, both of us sitting at Derek's feet. 'My girls,' Derek would say softly. In those moments I felt so safe.

Then I would have to haul myself up and go to work, leaving the two of them in their cocoon of contentment. I don't know where I heard that, but it was how they looked.

One day at the school, the woman I worked with looked at me in a knowing sort of way.

'What's his name?' she said. We had just finished polishing the long corridor. There was a new machine to do this and it was heavy, my wrists felt ready to snap.

'I said "what's his name?".'

'Who?'

'The man I saw you with the other day.'

'I don't know what you are talking about. I never go out.'

'Oh, come on. You can tell me.' She was staring at me, smiling, a dirty smile.

'It must have been someone else.'

'I don't think so,' she said, knowingly.

I didn't say any more, but after a while, when we had moved on to the next corridor, she said: 'You should be more careful. You're lucky it was me what saw you.'

I didn't think I was lucky. This woman was always telling me other people's secrets. As I walked home, I kept thinking about what she had said 'you should be more careful'. I didn't know how to be any more careful. I had always met Nick well away from Ely. It started to rain and even though I was so tired, I kept on walking, past the turn to where I lived and on into the town, then down to the river and along the towpath where the boats were moored. It was years since I had done this, I had been too frightened to go anywhere near when I was carrying Elizabeth in case Baz saw me and put two and two together. You never knew how men might be if they thought you might be having their baby. So I had just stopped going there and now it was as if the past twenty years hadn't happened. I was alone, in the dark, getting soaked through and looking to see if the boat was still there.

When I reached the place where I thought it had been, there was a boat but it didn't look the same. It was so silly, but I felt disappointed.

I turned back soon after passing it but I still wasn't ready to go home. I walked up through the town and paused to look in the windows of the charity shops but the lights were out and it was difficult to see much. One of the shops had a nice dress in the window and I thought I might go back in the morning, try it on. A few doors on there was a boutique with a couple of dresses in the window. I liked both of them a lot more than the other one.

When I got home and went in to Derek, he looked worried but he didn't get up.

'I thought something might have happened,' he said. Then: 'You're soaked. You must get a towel.'

'I sheltered for a while and then I couldn't hang

about any longer. Is Elizabeth home?'

'She's upstairs studying. She said you'd probably gone off to meet a friend.'

It made me feel uncomfortable the way Derek was looking at me, and just then I thought perhaps he knew. Then he said: 'Come here my darling and give me a kiss. I don't mind getting wet.'

I did what he asked and wondered whether this too meant that he knew.

Upstairs, I knocked on Elizabeth's door and went in. She didn't acknowledge me but that was not unusual. I asked her if she wanted anything. She shook her head without looking up from her studies.

I went to my room, grabbing a towel from the bathroom on the way. I sat down on the side of the bed and all the thoughts I didn't want rushed about in my head. I imagined Derek saying something to Elizabeth. The awful possibility of the woman I worked with spreading what she had seen. From now on I would be worrying all the time.

Chapter Forty-Two

Nick

C was pushing her luck. She wanted revenge and no doubt had hoped the court would send me to prison. When this didn't happen, I was relieved, of course, although my brief had told me it was highly unlikely I'd be banged up. I was relieved and at the same time glad to have seen the look on her face when I'd got away with it. I couldn't help smiling.

I felt the same sort of satisfaction in naming Tony in the divorce. C had been far too friendly with him for far too long, and even if they had not had sex, she had been unfaithful in a way. Besides, I had become tired of the way she had made it seem as if I was entirely to blame for our marriage ending. There was never an entirely innocent party in these things. C had allowed the marriage to go stale. She was as much to blame as I was.

I didn't want to think about it but I had to because I did not want to have to use lawyers any more than was absolutely necessary, the money they charge is obscene; so I did as much of the divorce work, or rather, the financial side of it, as I could. It was better this way. I saw no reason why I should let strangers see all the details of my business. I had every right to hold back in certain areas, which were also matters, if they came to light, that would implicate C, who had been a director. I was doing no more than protecting her. And Sophie. I still had to protect her. She would make a fuss if and when she found out I planned to leave the house and my assets to Simone, but I had spent a lot on her education and this had paid off, it wouldn't be long before she was earning a good salary and wouldn't need anything from me.

It was Simone who needed me now. It would be no more than a matter of time before she accepted that her future was with me. I had gone further than I really wanted in telling her she would have half the house and all the money, but at my age I had to be realistic. I could go back on the IE site, and I had looked once or twice after we'd been together and she had kept on avoiding making a decision; but there was no one else I wanted.

Sometimes I wondered whether my wanting her was partly because she was making herself unobtainable. She wasn't as clever as I'd hoped she might turn out to be, but did I want clever? I'd had that and it hadn't worked. It had turned out to be annoying, that's how I saw it now. Not that C had been all that clever, we wouldn't be in this situation if she had been. I had made it clear that she could go on living with me; after all, it was her home as much as it was mine, in some ways more so, as she was the one who had made it into a home, and I was grateful to her for that. But now that she had gone, it was not the same. I know, obviously it was not the same, you couldn't spend more than thirty years of your life with someone and not notice when they were no longer there. I don't think it was that I missed her. When she first went and there were the phone calls and emails, I felt something like disgust; she was in such a state, it was undignified and I hadn't expected that from her. She was allowing herself to wallow in whatever it was she was feeling and I didn't want to care. It was the only way, cut yourself off. Stop thinking about it. I should follow my own mantra.

One evening I noticed how quiet the house had become and it must have been very still outside. Suddenly it felt as if the place was contracting, stifling me. I thought about phoning Sophie, just for a chat, but I didn't really want to hear the reserve in her voice, the distance she had put between us. I could imagine the sort of conversations she had with her mother about me, not good. I was a total bastard. Ah, well.

I was restless. I walked around the house with no purpose. I thought of phoning Simone but this was not a good time for her to speak to me.

I did a bit of clearing up in the kitchen and tried to stop thinking. I paused after a while and looked out of the window, that amazing view over the town and then the fields beyond. All these years and I'd never stopped to take it in before, I was always too busy, building another business, preoccupied with whatever was going on. C had loved this about our kitchen, the view. I remember her saying so.

There was no more to do so I went back to the drawing room and turned on the television. It was University Challenge. I sat down and tried to clear my mind and concentrate on the questions. The first two rounds were ridiculously obscure. I got up and poured myself a brandy, it was a bottle I'd bought in France when I was with Simone.

The third round was worse than the first two and then in the fourth I got one, heard myself saying the answer out loud as I turned my head to the place where C always sat. I downed the brandy. A moment later I poured another.

'It's started,' C used to call to me.

We both used to get about the same number of answers right, which wasn't many. I couldn't imagine Simone knowing any.

Concentrate.

God, it was questions about literature, the ones C used to get.

More brandy.

I should have put water with it. My eyes were smarting.

Why didn't Sophie ever ring me?

Was C sitting in front of the new television she had taken when she left? Had she been able to answer the questions in that round?

Cosmology next!

I switched it off.

Silence.

I switched it on again.

Go for a drive.

Couldn't do that after two, three brandies on top of wine earlier.

There was always stuff to do in my study. It had been C's favourite room. She had chosen the paint colour and the wallpaper and the carpet and her desk had been in there until she got her job and it didn't make sense any more for me not to have the space to myself.

How about a cigar?

There was a box for them in the drawing room. C had bought it for me. On my way back to the study I picked up the brandy bottle and my glass.

I flicked on the PC screen and went to the emails. Nothing I hadn't already dealt with, except for a new piece of junk from the dating site. 'Welcome back,' it said.

It was a mistake to open that email. It didn't take many clicks to find that Simone was still there. Now I knew why she could see me only once a week. I took a long drag on the cigar and felt sick. I thought about the things I had bought for her, that ring. How many other men did she have giving her presents? I poured another brandy, this time filling the glass. I didn't need any water with it now.

I did some more clicks. Of course, there were no pictures and the brief descriptions failed to interest me. There was a car magazine on my desk. I began to flick through it but my mind was elsewhere. At this moment Simone could be with another man, in a hotel somewhere. I was still turning the pages of the magazine when the idea came to me, it was the method I had used many times before to come to a decision. The Ben Franklin Balance Sheet. Two lists, for and against, for and against Simone in this instance. Write down everything I could think of, add up the number in each column and decide based on how you felt about the result.

I started with the Cons: Unfaithful, indecisive, gold-digger, intellectually wanting, caused me to lose C, destroyed my relationship with Sophie, destroyed former social life, put the business at risk, made me look a fool. Pros: Sex, my age, her age, fondness. Love.

My head cleared. I did some searches online, found what I was looking for. It took a couple of hours, but the results looked passable. I forged Carys' signature and then took pictures of the documents I'd printed out. One handed over half the house, the other was part of a will. I emailed everything to Simone.

Chapter Forty-Three

I slept well that night. The brandy had done its job. But in the morning I had a bad head. I made a jug of strong coffee and downed a cup before going to my study to see if there was a reply from Simone. Nothing. But I was due to see her that afternoon. I would stop thinking about it and get on with some work, of which there was plenty. I was behind with stuff I needed to do for the business because so much of my time was taken up with the divorce.

Jerry came in mid-morning to moan about Carys telling him what to do. This was a constant issue and tiresome. Both were good at what they did but had never got on. Each liked to think they were second-in-command to me. It had always been a delicate balancing act.

This morning Jerry wanted to tell me something about Charlotte. It annoyed me that he still saw her but on the other hand he was able to let me know what she was up to. C had always been too open with people, which was how Jerry knew about my affair. I had hoped she might have been more circumspect, it would have been more dignified for her to let people think we had simply parted; there had been no need to mention a third party.

Jerry waffled on about one or two maintenance matters before coming to the point, that C had asked him to go over to her place to fix something and the chat they'd had.

'D'you know her cousin?'

'Clive?'

'That's the one. He's offered to have you done over, Nick.'

Jerry, standing in front of my desk, had managed to adopt a look of concern but I could see he was relishing being the bearer of this piece of nonsense. I also knew that C was intelligent enough to appreciate that if anything untoward happened to me, she would be the first person to come under suspicion, albeit someone else had 'done me over'.

I laughed. 'I don't think so.'

'Listen, mate. I'm just telling you.'

I hated it when he called me 'mate'.

'Okay, Jerry. I hear you.'

'This Clive. What's he like?'

'All mouth.'

Jerry looked a little deflated.

'That's all right, then.'

'Pretty much.' I paused. 'But thanks for telling me.'

That afternoon, as I drove to meet Simone, it occurred to me that C had told Jerry because she knew he would tell me and perhaps I should be careful. Clive had boasted in the past about the people he knew, people who owed him favours, who liked 'doing people over'. It wouldn't hurt, I decided, to increase security at the house. I also decided I wouldn't say anything about this nonsense to Simone in case it frightened her. I realised that I wanted to protect her. Her vulnerability was part of the attraction. I wanted her to be free from the drudgery of her life with a sick husband, no money and a daughter, who, from what I could tell, had little regard for her. And if the documents I had emailed to her the previous night didn't do the trick I didn't know what else would. Did she love me at all? Had I read her all wrong? I sensed that today was going to be crunch time.

Chapter Forty-Four

Charlotte

I loved my cousin but I knew he was a rogue, morals were not his thing. Yet he had been outraged by the way Nick had behaved and when he offered to have Nick hurt for hurting me, I was going through the mental brick-throwing phase and the idea appealed. But only for a split second, so I laughed. Clive didn't and I realised he had meant what he said. It also occurred to me that he relished the possibility of putting into action a piece of violence, and it turned out he had never liked Nick, had always thought him a shit.

I don't know why I told Jerry about the threat. Was it to warn Nick or to frighten him? I think it was just another example of me being too open, telling all whenever I could. But at last this was coming to an end, it had to before it became boring, yesterday's news. And I no longer wanted to talk about it, so that when my friends asked what was happening, I said things like 'getting there', 'nothing to report', even though there always was.

I still thought about it all more than was healthy, I couldn't stop, but it no longer hurt as much. I had begun to feel hopeful in a way that had nothing to do with Nick. It was innate optimism. It was there and I recognised it as a shift towards the future rather than the past.

'I am a friend of Derek Rolls,' the email began.

'His wife has left him and gone to live with your husband. Derek is distraught and would like to talk to you. If you feel you can do this, here is his number.'

What did I feel when I read this? I can't pretend it didn't stir things up again. Nick had got what he wanted. Simone was now living in my house, surrounded by the things inherited from my family, the things Nick and I had accumulated together over thirty years. I know, things shouldn't matter, but they sharpen the feeling of displacement.

Should I speak to Derek Rolls? I felt sorry for him, he was only just starting out on the horrible experience I had been through. I wanted to help him, if I could, although of course I couldn't. He probably needed to know more, just as I had been compelled to extract cruel detail from Nick. I also wanted to know more about Simone, what sort of person she was, how she had managed to take Nick from me. I knew very little about her, other than that she had a daughter and, Nick had said, worked in marketing.

I resisted calling Derek Rolls for all of six hours. When I got home from work, I dialled the number. The man who answered sounded old and shaky.

'I really do appreciate this,' he said. 'Can you tell me what you know?'

So I had to go through the story again before Derek told me what had happened.

'I had to go to the hospital for a check-up. Heart problems.' He made a hollow-sounding laugh at this. 'She would normally come with me but I knew she was tired. I think she wanted to come with me.' He paused, his voice breaking a little.

'When I got home, she had gone. She had taken all her clothes, but she left her laptop. I don't know whether she meant to. Betty, that's our daughter, knew the password and found some documents giving half your house to her mother, and a will. Your husband seems to have given her everything.'

'Doesn't she know he's not in a position to do that?' I was furious.

'Simone is not very educated or sophisticated.'

'But she's got a good job?'

'She works in a school and in some offices. She gets very tired.'

'Does she teach marketing at evening classes?'

'She doesn't teach anything. She's a cleaner. That's how we met. She came to clean for my mother and me, years ago. We both became fond of her and when Mother died, well, I don't know what I would have done without her. I don't know what I am going to do without her now.'

'How is your daughter taking it?' I asked.

'Badly. She says she hates her mother but I don't want that.'

'And your check-up, how did it go?'

'Not the best, but all I can think about is losing Simone. I shall miss her terribly. I didn't think she had such cruelty in her.'

'They are both cruel, then,' I said. 'Nick can be so charming but there is another side to him. We used to argue a lot, which I hated, but I think he liked it, and when I wouldn't answer back any more, he turned to our daughter, Sophie. I didn't know it, but she told me recently that he used to make her cry every afternoon when he fetched her from school. I felt so awful about not knowing. It was monstrous, the way he treated her.' You say these things in the heat of the moment and then it's on to something else.

Derek said he would like us to meet. This I had to think about, but before I could decide, something else happened.

I'd never been active on Facebook, but when something appears which relates to something you've said, it doesn't take long to hear about it, one way or another. Nick's email said he was withdrawing the offer to lend me the money for my house and that he would make sure I got nothing. He had seen what I had said about him, that he was a monster who had been cruel to his children. Simone's daughter had made the post and it had been seen by Simone's sister.

I didn't know what to do. I spoke to my brother about it. He had said all along that it was better not to rattle Nick and that I was not to have any further contact with Simone's husband.

This, of course, made sense, but I felt it was all wrong that I couldn't say what I wanted and that I had now been put in the wrong for doing so. I was like a wasp buzzing against a windowpane. And then I thought about Sophie and how she would feel when she saw the post, as I knew she would. What had I done?

For months, my brother had done his best to negotiate a settlement on my behalf so that I didn't have to spend everything I had on solicitors' fees. Now he was furious with me. Charles never lost his temper but I could tell how angry he was. I must never speak to Simone's husband again, it was far too dangerous.

As I said, I don't 'do' Facebook, its banality makes me feel gloomy, and after what happened via its platform, I hated it with unreasonable fervour. The daughter had told the world what I had said to her father about Nick. He was a monster who had been cruel to his child, was the truncated version. There was truth in this but I didn't think I had used the word 'monster' - 'cruel', yes.

Not being able to say what I liked was another injustice I'd have to wrestle with. I don't know what Charles said to Nick but somehow he managed to smooth things over, or so it seemed. I had great faith in my brother but as more months went by and progress towards a settlement just didn't seem to be happening, I realised that Nick was playing the delay game. Charles was negotiating in good faith and perhaps did not realise how Nick could justify to himself any amount of bad faith to achieve what he considered was duly his. I'd had more than thirty years to see this at close quarters and I knew I had added a further dollop of 'justification' by speaking to Simone's husband. But that was me, too open. I felt like a child who had blurted out a truth that should not have been said and was being punished for it.

As well as the Facebooked version of what I'd

said to Derek, his daughter had added pictures of the documents Nick had sent to Simone. They painted a picture of a gold-digger, and in my guileless state this was how I saw it for a long time. I also thought how desperate Nick must have been to get Simone to leave her husband. I didn't know the half of it.

Sophie, of course, did Facebook, she was too young not to, and this was how she found out she had been disinherited. And it wasn't the money that upset her but the injustice.

I had decided from the start that I could not say anything bad about Nick to Sophie, it wouldn't be fair. It was different with Vicky, I could speak freely about her step-father, but the need to do so had faded, it was like poking a fire that should be left to go out. I was also aware that I could no longer burden Vicky or anyone else with my off-loadings about Nick.

So, what could I say to Sophie when she railed against her father for his unfairness to her? I said he must be desperate.

I thought then about what my doctor had said about Nick, that he would be a lonely old man. I thought about the time Nick and I had talked in the pressing stillness of our drawing room after his confession, talked about the future when there didn't seem to be one. Neither of us had ever lived alone, we had said, and neither of us wanted to. I realised we were both frightened and this was why we had considered Mrs Clark.

When we were still talking, hadn't Nick told me he had thought about the possibility of both Simone and

Derek moving in with him, the house was big enough.
That was desperate.

Chapter Forty-Five

Simone

Elizabeth wanted to go to a festival once with her friends and when she asked me if she could have the money to pay for it, I had to say no, there just wasn't any spare. The look on her face said too much. She stared at me for a moment or two, disappointment, dislike. I felt such a failure. I wondered whether she had already asked Derek and could imagine how he too would have to let her down, but I doubted she would have shown him the same face.

It stayed with me, my daughter's disappointment. The next time I saw Nick I told him, perhaps thinking he might offer to lend me the money, although how would I ever be able to pay it back? He listened to me but said nothing. Later, when we were getting dressed, he told me that Elizabeth should be able to go to as many festivals as she liked and that I knew what to do.

The day Derek went to the hospital for his check-up, I bundled my clothes into bin bags and waited for Nick to come. I was so nervous I jumped at every sound. When the post was pushed through the letterbox, the thump on the mat made my heart race and my head fuzz. I was sweating in my armpits. I kept going to the window to watch for his car and one time I looked up and saw the woman who lived opposite staring back at me. She quickly let the net curtain fall back in place but I was sure she was still looking. Then I thought what did it matter? We would never see each other again. I didn't have to worry anymore.

Nick was taking his time, I had expected him long before this and I began to think he could have changed his mind. I had said I would go and live with him but maybe he was the sort of man who lost interest as soon as he got what he wanted. I didn't really know him at all. I looked at the row of bin bags, full of the charity shop dresses I had bought over the years. If Nick did come, I would never go in another shop like that, never.

Then my phone rang. I grabbed it, thinking it must be Nick, about to say 'where are you?' It was the woman I worked with at the school. She would be a bit late in the morning, she said. This was the third or fourth time she had done this and the last time she had not turned up until I had nearly finished. I thought it was possible the school would not get cleaned tomorrow.

I was in the bathroom when the knock came and something in me said don't rush and don't expect it to be Nick.

When I opened the door, he was standing there, red-faced, looking grumpy.

'What took you so long?' He sounded as annoyed as he looked. I could have asked him the same question but decided against.

'Are your bags ready to go in the car?'

I nodded, then looked at him and suddenly his face changed. I think it was relief. Perhaps he'd thought I might have changed my mind.

Together we loaded the bags into the car, and then I saw the net curtain across the road move a little and suddenly I wanted to laugh.

I think Nick was now as nervous as I had been; he started the car and we raced down to the main road as if something or somebody might try to stop us.

Neither of us spoke on the journey to his house, which was now my house too. What was happening seemed unreal to me, that I had done something so wrong but it didn't feel bad. I told myself I had done it for Elizabeth, so she could have all she wanted and it was through me she would get it, not Derek.

I was sad about Derek. I didn't want to make him unhappy but I doubted I had ever made him that happy, I had just been someone who was there.

Perhaps it started to become more real when I opened the wardrobe to hang up my dresses and found it was already half full of Nick's wife's clothes. They were mainly black, and huge. Without thinking about it too much, I took them off their hangers and after I had taken my own clothes from the bin bags, I stuffed what I had found into them. I didn't know what else to do. It seemed a bit odd Nick had left them there. All sorts of thoughts were coming into my head and one of them, the one that stuck, was that Nick still expected his wife to return one day, and then he would take back everything he said he had given to me. Thinking beyond this was more than I could do. I decided not to say anything that might annoy him.

Over the next day or so, he spent a lot of time in his study so I hardly saw him until the evening. Then we would cook something and after we had eaten, he wanted us to sit together on the settee and watch television, programmes I didn't understand and found boring. He was affectionate to me, his arm round my shoulders, and I thought this felt better than sitting on the floor with my head in Derek's lap, watching television sideways.

I tried not to think too much about Elizabeth and Derek but when I couldn't stop, I thought perhaps Elizabeth would forgive me one day. I didn't know how, but if I could start giving her things, that might help.

Nick wanted to give me things. He said we would go shopping together and buy me new clothes. This gave me a warm feeling and I snuggled into him.

He didn't really start talking until my sister sent a text message telling me to look on my daughter's Facebook page if I wanted to see what sort of man I had run off with and asking why I hadn't told her and Mama what I was doing.

We went to his study, I hadn't been in this room before. It had a long window overlooking the driveway. There was a fireplace and a cupboard and shelves built into the wall either side. There was a big old desk with a computer screen on it, and a swivel chair with a high back. Nick sat down in it and I stood beside him as he clicked on Facebook and then asked me to look for what my sister was talking about.

There was a picture of Derek and Elizabeth, their heads touching, looking sad, and then the words said to Derek by Nick's wife about Nick being a monster who was cruel to his children.

'What a bitch,' he kept saying. 'What a bitch.' His face had gone all red and his eyes so dark and threatening.

'She won't get a penny, not now, and I'll sue her for defamation.'

It upset me, his anger, and I started to get confused.

'You won't sue Elizabeth, will you?'

'Don't be ridiculous,' he said nastily.

'I'm sorry.'

'It's better you keep out of this. Let me deal with it. You've done enough already.'

'What have I done?'

'You've split my family, if you really want to know.'

'But I thought this was what you wanted.'

'You're joking! I didn't want this mess. I would have been happy going on as we were if C hadn't found out.'

'I thought you wanted me.'

'I did. I do. Why do women always want things to be so black and white?'

I didn't understand. I must have looked blank. I felt numb. Nick was watching me now and suddenly his face changed again, back to how I liked it. He stood up and grabbed hold of me, wrapped his arms round me and kissed the top of my head.

'I'm sorry,' he said.

Chapter Forty-Six

Charlotte

It was a great relief to me, Sophie's lack of concern about what I had said and its reporting on Facebook. I thought it possible there might be a part of her that was glad the misery she'd endured had been put out there. She loved her father but had always been ready to stand up to him, especially when he turned nasty in their arguments and went off into the realms of illogicality; she just wouldn't let him get away with it. There was enough of him in her to fight back even if it made her cry in frustration. And, like me, she knew the side to him which was difficult not to love.

'To my beautiful C. You have given me the best present I could ever have,' he wrote on the card with my Christmas present the year Sophie was born.

'I was good after Sophie was born,' he had said when I found out about Simone and all the others, all the others I had never known about. 'I was good for a long time.'

In retrospect this sounds more like endurance than choice. 'Good' because his sexual activity was confined to me.

But he was good. He shared the care of our baby, and with pleasure not forbearance. And he was always kind to Vicky whereas he could have been indifferent as she was not his. I don't think he ever put a foot wrong with Vicky and she was fond of him, but when the moment came, she simply went cold on him. He was not her father and he had done his best to destroy me.

It is hard to remember the good times, although in all those years there must have been many, as I don't remember being unhappy apart from when he changed into the red-faced, steely-eyed unreachable, but even then I always retained a sense of permanence in our relationship and that we both felt the same way.

'But you and Nick are special,' that friend had said when she heard what had happened. I thought so.

Just as he could switch from loving to loathsome and back again, the same happened over the Facebook post. Perhaps Simone calmed him, I can't possibly know, but his anger went and whatever my brother had said to him did the trick. And after all the months of uncertainty, it seemed as if I was getting somewhere despite my stupidity.

I made a huge loss on the house in France but what I got was enough, along with the reinstated loan agreement with Nick, to go ahead with buying the house I was living in. It was tiny compared with the house I had left. Friends had said I should not have left, that he should have gone, and they were probably right, but these things tend not to be so straightforward when they are happening.

I didn't contact Derek Rolls again, there really was no point and there was always the danger I would say something that could be used against me. I didn't see Amit again either, and was a bit sad about that, sad because that spark he had been in my life had simply vanished.

Now I was properly on my own and it was okay. I had been so desperate not to be alone because I never had been. 'I don't want to live alone,' I had said to Nick. 'Neither do I,' he'd said.

Of course, I wasn't alone. I had my family and my friends, and there was a lodger in my spare room; but I did not have a partner and perhaps I didn't want one. I knew from my first marriage that it was possible to be lonely while you were with someone. I had never felt lonely with Nick, and now it wasn't loneliness being away from him, it was what Adam had said, I was free. Grasping what this meant had been impossible for me when he had said it, all I could feel then was confusion, my whole world tipped over and survival the overriding instinct.

I had always known it would take time to recover and accepted this might never fully be the case. And then something new happened.

Chapter Forty-Seven

Nick

Wanting something or someone can consume your life until you get it. I was relieved to be able to concentrate on the business again after Simone had come to live with me. She was quiet and unobtrusive, let me get on with what I had to do and managed to busy herself in the house. There were no complaints, she wasn't like that, but she looked sad when she didn't realise I was looking and I suppose this was because of her daughter. Winning round Elizabeth would have to be my next project, but it seemed like a good idea to let things settle for a while.

At first she didn't want to leave the house without me, and there was no need, groceries were ordered online and then the new clothes I wanted for her. We didn't go out at night. We watched television but not until later as I stayed in my study until nine. She didn't mind which programmes we watched and I couldn't tell whether the ones I chose interested her. The inscrutability which had drawn me to her was fundamental, not adopted.

We were watching Newsnight when something happened. There was a loud bang on the window and then the sound of it cracking.

'Lie on the floor,' I shouted at her as I went to pull back the curtain. It was too dark outside to see anything, but the window pane was fractured, something heavy had hit it hard.

Was Clive my first or second thought? I went across the room to turn out the lights and then back to the window to look out across the garden. Everything out there was still, as far as I could see, there wasn't even any wind, the trees static.

I looked round to Simone, prone on the carpet, her head to one side. She was looking at me with a mixture of fear and curiosity, she wanted to know what I would do. My instinct was to leave well alone and have a scout round in the morning but I could see this would not look good. It occurred to me that if someone was out there, they could have thrown whatever it was at the window in order to bring me outside.

'Don't go out there,' she whispered. 'Don't leave me alone.'

I don't think either of us slept very well that night and for the first time since she had come to live with me, we did not have sex. I got up early and went to inspect the damage. Lying on the ground by the window was an owl. I went in, Simone had come down and I told her. I laughed and went to embrace her but she drew away.

'I'm frightened,' she said.

'But it was only a bird.'

'I know, but it made me feel threatened. I can't explain.'

I looked at her. She seemed genuinely upset.

'I'm sorry. I should have had a look when it happened. You've had all night to dwell on it, haven't you?' Then she let me hold her.

I didn't think any further about the bird and the cracked pane but it seemed to have a lasting effect on Simone. She was jumpy if there was a sudden sound, anxious if there was someone at the front door, and this seemed to get worse. After a few days, I sat her down and said we needed to talk about the way she felt.

'I've done something very wrong and I will have to pay.'

'What do you mean?'

'You know what I am saying. We have both behaved as we shouldn't. I feel so guilty, and ashamed. Perhaps I should go back, and you should ask your wife to come home.'

'Don't be ridiculous. These things happen all the time. You shouldn't feel you are entirely in the wrong. It takes two, you know, to make a marriage work.' I could see she was not convinced. She was probably thinking about her daughter. She was also looking at me in a way I found irritating, as if I could provide her with an answer that would make everything neat and tidy.

'You must do what you think best,' I said, standing up. 'But don't assume that your husband and daughter will welcome you back with open arms. They will never trust you again.' Perhaps I had gone too far, but I couldn't deal with this new uncertainty, I'd put up with it for months while she had dilly-dallied about what to do.

She continued to sit there, her hands in her lap, her head down, and said no more.

I went to my study and closed the door. Sitting at my desk, I began to feel angry. I had given up a great deal to be with Simone. Unless I was careful, I was going to lose half the business, half the house. C had been a fool to leave, I'd been seeing Simone for months without her suspecting a thing, we could have continued like that until the affair fizzled out and she'd have been none the wiser. There was a bitter taste in my mouth.

As I've always said, it is better not to think about these things too much, and Simone said no more about going back to her husband. But something had been lost. It was probably just that first intoxication which can never last; even so, I missed it.

I had not expected Simone's husband to come after me for money but that's what he did. He wanted a quarter of the value of my house and maintenance. I couldn't believe it. What sort of a man was he? Didn't he have any pride?

The last thing I wanted was more legal expenses and I doubted he could afford any from what Simone had told me. The best idea seemed to be to have a meeting, the three of us, and sort out a nominal amount to make him go away. I wasn't sure he'd agree to see me, but he said he would and suggested a hotel, fortunately not one where Simone and I had been.

Simone was nervous about the idea. She was nervous about everything now, didn't want me to leave her alone in the house day or night, and as she didn't like going out, this meant we were becoming virtually housebound. All I could hope was she would get over this neurosis in time.

The meeting with Rolls was arranged, it was to be in one of those big anonymous hotels near the airport. I couldn't read what Simone was thinking. I'd quite expected her to refuse to come, but she said nothing, just got in the car, strapped herself in and stared ahead.

'It'll be fine,' I said as we turned out of the drive.

'Who for?'

'For all of us.'

'How can you know?'

'Don't ask stupid questions.' I hoped there would be no more discussion until we were with Rolls. I had already told her what I planned to do and as she had not come up with anything else, it was better she kept quiet.

I was curious to meet Rolls, to find out what sort of a man he was. It had been the same all those years ago when I had gone to C's house to meet her husband. I hoped Rolls would be as dignified as he had been, although asking for maintenance from your estranged wife was hardly that.

We found a parking space close to the entrance and then I thought better of it and drove to a more secluded spot, I didn't want Rolls to see the car and assume he could extract more money from me. As we walked back towards the hotel entrance and the doors parted, Simone hung back, a few steps behind me.

'Come on, keep up, I don't know what he looks like.'

I had turned to her and now she was looking beyond

me. Rolls was sitting in a corner. My first impression was of a man without any physical attraction. His clothes looked creased and dirty and I don't think he had shaved that morning. Perhaps this look was deliberate.

I went over to him and offered my hand, which he took, although he did not stand up. Simone was very nervous; as she sat down, I noticed her hands trembling in her lap. I saw her glance at Rolls and then look away, while he carried on looking at her until I suggested we order coffee. He looked at me and smiled. Then his attention was back on Simone.

'How are you, my darling?'

I felt he had no right to speak to her in this way, not any more. It hardened my resolve to screw him down to the lowest sum, even shame him into going away empty-handed.

'Let's get down to business,' I said. 'I've done some research and I don't think you are entitled to anything, but I am prepared to make a goodwill gesture and offer you £25,000. This would be on the understanding that you make no further claim.'

The coffee arrived and Rolls took his cup, sipped from it and slowly put it back on the saucer. Then he looked straight at me and shook his head.

'The offer is likely to go down if we start horse-trading,' I said, calling his bluff.

'You think so?'

'I know so.'

'The courts are a lot more even-handed these days. If the sole provider leaves and comes into money, what do you think the result will be?'

'You'll have to excuse me,' I said, getting up. In the toilet I took my time. I needed a minute or two to think about my next move, although I didn't like leaving Simone alone with Rolls. But when I returned, it was as if neither of them had moved an inch or said anything. Simone's gaze was down and Rolls was still looking at her, although his expression had changed, hardened, I thought.

I touched Simone's shoulder and indicated she should get up, which she did. I turned to Rolls.

'We'll see you in court, then.' This time I did not offer my hand.

Chapter Forty-Eight

Charlotte

It seemed as if there would be no end to my financial worries. The proposed legal loan was now uppermost in my mind. It suggested to me that my solicitor thought I might end up with nothing. Nick and I knew of a couple who had fought over the money for seven years until all of it had gone on legal fees, certainly as far as the wife was concerned, although we both suspected the husband had a substantial stash somewhere. I was sure Nick would be thinking he could pull off the same trick.

And then I had an email from Derek Rolls. He said he was planning to take Simone to court, that he had no choice. He said he had had a meeting with them, in a hotel, and that when Nick had gone to the loo, Simone had told him she was unhappy and wanted to come back.

As I read this I realised that I was losing interest in what might happen, that it no longer concerned me, other than financially. If Derek Rolls succeeded in his claim, I had to believe the amount would be decided on Nick's half of our assets and not mine. This was the way I was thinking; only later did it cross my mind that if Simone went back to her husband, Nick might want me to return.

I think it's cruel the way legal process takes so long. You're left in limbo and as much as you try to get on with your life, the 'unfinished business' feeling taints everything. You don't know where it is going to end.

I was still on the dating site and had met a man who seemed to like me. I didn't hold out any hope of romance, I don't think I wanted that, not any more. I'd had my wild time, and enjoyed it, but you can have too much of a good thing. I think I was beginning to appreciate what being free really meant, it wasn't about going out with lots of different men, it was about being able to choose what to do without having to consider anyone else. Vicky and Sophie had their own lives now, they did not need me day-to-day, hadn't for some while.

Freedom can be empty and I suppose that was how it felt when Adam first pointed it out to me, but mine was filling up – with the things I now did with friends and never really had when I was with Nick - and the times when I was alone I was happy to be so. If I'm honest, I knew I would never fully get over what had happened but it was no longer heartbreak, just the scar of having been rejected. They say life is too short but it is also not long enough to completely recover.

The new man in my life came to the pub on Friday nights. He didn't say a lot, just fitted in, and then we would go back to my house and have coffee and talk about I don't know what before I said I was going to bed and he left. This suited me fine, I had a new friend who was easy to be with, undemanding. I could talk to him about anything. I asked him what he thought about the legal loan.

My wonderful old school friend, who had given up a night at the opera to come to me the time I lost it in a big way, had offered to lend me some money and while logically it was more than likely I would be able to pay her back in due course, it was the length of the due course that worried me. We could all be dead before due course had gone its way.

My new man offered to lend me money too, but I couldn't take that either. Neither he nor my friend had any idea how much my legal costs might amount to, and neither did I. But I was now certain that Nick intended to drain me of all funds, just the way the husband in the couple we knew had done to his wife.

The new man had offered me his money before he told me he loved me. I didn't take this too seriously, perhaps because the last time I'd heard it was when Nick had said it was possible to love two people at the same time, instantly devaluing the whole notion. Besides, I did not love the new man. I liked him, which seemed enough in a relationship which had settled into the weekly pattern of Friday nights.

Meanwhile I had to think about taking the legal loan, although every time I got close to signing the form, I baulked at the frightening interest rate. Mulling it over, I kept coming back to Nick and how he hated lawyers and paying too much for things. And then I would think about him some more and remember times when we were up against it together, and how during those times we had been at our closest.

Chapter Forty-Nine

Simone

Seeing Derek again made me feel more confused. I realised how much I missed his kindness and had depended on it for so long. But asking him to take me back was a big mistake. I didn't blame him for saying no, and if I had stayed quiet, I might have been able to go back to him eventually. I had thought Nick had kindness but now I realised he used it only when he wanted me to agree to something.

I thought more and more about Elizabeth and it got more painful not seeing or speaking to her. I sent her some money but heard nothing back. I bought things for her online. Nick kept saying she would come round in time, but he didn't know her or how much she loved Derek, how little she thought of me. And what I had done could only make this worse.

What I had to do was remember how hard it had been, no money, cleaning the school and the offices, the months of hating myself for being a cheat. But now I wished I had never gone on the dating site and when I thought about it, I couldn't understand how I had let myself. I felt dirty.

After a while I realised that this was how Nick felt about me, dirty. It had to be that. It was why he was so nasty to me. From what he had said, I felt he had never wanted his wife to leave and that he blamed me even though we had done it together. I felt insecure. I thought that if his wife said she wanted to come back, he would let her. This worried me so much I had to ask him about the financial stuff he said he had done, the giving me half the house and everything in his will. I tried to wait for a good moment but it never seemed to come, and I was frightened how he would be if I asked him.

It kept going round in my head until I no longer believed he had given me so much. I had never seen the actual documents but how could I ask?

I felt like a prisoner in Nick's house. There was nothing to stop me from going out but I had lost all my confidence. One day I had made myself go out alone. I went down into the town to look in the shop windows, the way I had liked to when I first went to live at Mrs Rolls' house. There were lots of charity shops in the high street and I was standing outside one, admiring a dress, when I sensed that I was being stared at. I carried on looking at the dress and in the reflection of the window I could see two women across the street, their heads close together and glancing over towards me. This was a small town, there probably weren't many people who looked like me. The women could be friends of Nick's wife. Suddenly I felt terribly exposed. I wanted to run back to the house, close the door, close out the town that knew Charlotte and would never want to know me.

I managed to walk, not run and I didn't look at the two women. I didn't want to see what I suspected would be in their faces, how much they knew, how much they had been told.

I didn't know how to carry on. Living with Nick did not feel like forever. I tried to remember what it had been like when we were just dating, what we had talked about, but it was just silence, I couldn't find the memory. He didn't talk to me much now. When he did, it was about the people who worked for him. Carys was a lazy cow, he said, Jerry was a creep, others were stupid and greedy, useless, brainless, fat.

Fat seemed to be what he disliked most, it went with greedy and lazy and stupid. It was "most unattractive" he would say, as if warning me not to go there, not to become like his wife, not to let myself go. I'd never had to think about my weight but now that I had no work, I had noticed that some of my clothes were a bit tight. I was eating too many chocolates but the more I tried to stop, the harder it was to leave them alone. I spent a lot of time sitting by myself in the kitchen, thinking about Elizabeth, wondering what she was doing, sometimes imagining how it would be if she forgave me. I could almost feel happy in these thoughts, just for a moment or two.

When Nick told me Sophie was coming to the house, I thought he wouldn't want me there but he didn't say this. I had no idea where I could go but I told him I would go out. He got cross then.

'Don't be stupid. You've got to meet her sooner or later. This is her home.'

I wondered whether it would ever feel like mine. The only things in this house which belonged to me were my clothes. All the things surrounding me were what Nick and his wife had chosen, just as all the things in Mrs Rolls' house had been hers. I had nothing.

The day Sophie came, I stayed in the bedroom. I wasn't ready to meet her. I knew she must hate me. I didn't want to see that in her eyes.

After she'd gone, I heard Nick coming upstairs. I began to feel frightened, he'd be angry with me. He would say I was stupid.

I quickly hid the chocolates before he came into the bedroom. He didn't say anything at first and I couldn't read his face, whether he was going to be nasty to me.

He came towards the bed and sat down beside me, his hands on his knees, staring at the floor.

'This is no good,' he said. 'You've upset Sophie. She wanted to meet you, I'm sure she did. Why didn't you come downstairs?' His voice was even. He was either very cross or just disappointed. I couldn't think of anything to say.

We sat like that for a while. Perhaps he was waiting for me to explain. Perhaps I should say I was sorry, but that didn't explain. I felt so lonely.

Chapter Fifty

Nick

Before I started sitting in the chair rather than on the sofa next to C, there was something she did to me if I had said something she found amusing. She called it spifflication. She would round on me and tickle me vigorously. I was never sure whether I liked it, it was almost too intimate, and I am extremely ticklish. I would try and push her off but being tickled makes you laugh, so it was mixed messages.

Perhaps that was the problem all along, mixed messages. I'm pretty sure there were times in the marriage when she didn't love me enough and this was certainly how I felt about her sometimes. Then she would do something to start it all up again, like being over-friendly with another man who I could see would be up for it if she gave him the chance. I'd want her even though I was annoyed with her.

We used to go to a fair number of parties and it was usually on these occasions the being over-friendly would happen. Leaving aside this, I was never sure how much I enjoyed these gatherings. They could be tedious, silly, instantly forgettable small-talk. I didn't mind talking about cars, but none of our friends had a car as top-of-the-range as mine and I did not really want to hear about what they were driving. If this sounds elitist of whatever, I'm sorry, but that's how it was. Why pretend interest? Why should I? For the sake of appearances? It didn't matter.

It was mostly the same people we met at these dos, a hard core of party-goers, the men boring, the women drunk. Jane was the worst, although I still had a soft spot for her. She was the only one I missed from that crowd, all of whom had slipped out of my life like disappearing vapour after C left. But I didn't really care. How can you regret losing the company of boring people?

I had never felt that I needed friends; self-sufficiency was one of my assets, although I can't pretend it was all that pleasant living alone. I'd always been certain I would be able to persuade Simone to eventually leave her husband. I just hadn't known how long it might take, whether we really would have to wait until he died. I don't feel it was wrong to consider that, it wasn't as if either of us was willing it, he was doing that himself with his appalling life-style.

When you are as taken with somebody as I was with Simone, you will put up with quite a lot. It's like being ravenously hungry. Then you get to eat all you want and that hunger goes.

One day, some time after things had settled down, at least for the moment – I was still fighting C on the divorce front but that was going to continue for a very long time unless she became sensible – I had gone into town to the post office. Jane was in the queue. She didn't see me and it crossed my mind to leave it that way, doubtless C had told her what a bastard I was; but Jane, I remembered, liked a bastard, she'd married two of them.

She readily agreed to an early lunchtime drink, and never one to hold back, she hugged me and said she was glad we were still friends.

In the pub, I looked at her as she rattled on about nobody knowing what went on inside a marriage and who was anyone else to judge, and that C had rather let herself go. However, the way she looked now was incredible, wasn't it. I looked at her and thought about fucking her again.

Before we parted, she said she would like to meet Simone. She added that she had not wanted to be disloyal to C, which was a joke considering the sex she had enjoyed with me in the past, but now that it had been a while since C had left, she didn't see why we shouldn't have a get-together, the four of us.

Jane's third husband was one of the car bores, but I didn't dislike him. He was harmless and more accommodating than was reasonable when it came to Jane's excesses. When she had had too much to drink, which was frequent, he would gather her up and with soothing words take her home as she threw unpleasant words at him.

I thought I might hear from her soon after our chance meeting, but she didn't make contact, so I sent her a text, inviting her and her husband to come to the house for drinks. There was no reply and for some reason this annoyed me, so I sent the text again, adding that I had sent it before and assumed it must have gone astray. The reply that came was not what I expected, not after our drink together and her saying she wanted to meet Simone. They were busy and could not commit to anything.

It was her husband, it had to be. And C. God knows what she had told them. All of them could go to hell as far as I was concerned. The upside was it strengthened my resolve to keep fighting C until she ran out of money and had to settle for whatever I decided to let her have.

Chapter Fifty-One

Charlotte

I had not expected to hear from Derek Rolls again, but one evening he rang me. He said he had taken Simone to court and had lost. He sounded strangely unconcerned about this. Then he told me how after the hearing he had been outside the court with Nick and Simone and had asked them to give him a lift home.

'My barrister – he's an old friend – looked astounded when the three of us drove off together. But I'm glad I asked because it gave me an opportunity to observe the relationship, and there isn't one.'

Wishful thinking? Perhaps. I asked him how he was getting on. He told me he had met someone new, that he had paid her air fare from Thailand and they had spent a blissful time together. He added that his daughter Betty had liked her too, best of best friends, so lovely to see.

I wondered how he had been able to afford an air fare, but wasn't about to ask.

'The bit you will like is that your husband paid for it all. Simone puts money in Betty's bank account, but Betty won't take it and gives it to me!'

How much did this sting? Half of this was my money and at a time when, if I'd had any spare cash, I would have liked to give it to Sophie, who was struggling in London. I didn't think she was getting any money from her father, not now she had a job, but she wasn't earning very much. That Simone's daughter was benefitting, even if she chose to give the money to her father, was a hard one.

I shouldn't have done what I did next. I called Sophie and told her about the money going to the daughter. I wanted to know if she was getting any sort of allowance. And Sophie, being the straightforward person she is, called Nick.

'You did that to turn Sophie against me,' Nick spat down the phone. 'You can forget about any sort of divorce settlement, now or in the future. You know I can make this go on for years, and I will.'

Money worries are wretched. They drag you down but at the same time you feel it's somehow wrong to fret too much about your material wellbeing; other things could be so much worse, and, for me, the rest of my life was okay, more than that really, I had told my friend that I loved him, and I did.

It was an entirely different sort of love from what I could remember of falling in love with Nick, which had been against my better judgement, judgement I had felt but chosen to suppress in that heady state of desire.

I could see the possibility of lasting contentment and it was extremely attractive.

With Nick I had realised pretty quickly that things were going to be difficult and there had been times over our long marriage when I had fallen out of love with him; it was just bad luck that when he fell out of love with me, I was back in love with him. I was content then. My mistake had been to think he was too.

When I'd left, he had given me that warning, not to back him into that corner, which was probably where he felt he was now and to him justified his determination to fight me to the last penny. And to keep control, which, even if he didn't know it, was what he always wanted.

I had been blind to this, but others had not. Charles said he and Mary had been concerned for some years about the way Nick controlled Sophie. Perhaps he had while he could, but Sophie was not the sort of person to be controlled by anyone, which was doubtless why they had fought so much. The grown-up Sophie still loved her father but she had distanced herself from him, she was no longer interested in arguing with him, she found it tedious. She was angry with him for being unfair over money, but her way was to get on with making it for herself.

My situation was precarious. I no longer had any earning power. Retirement had come, my pension was pitiful. The plan had been for it to come from the business. I had put what little money I'd had all those years ago into the company and if I had been no more than an investor, my original stake would still be worth enough for me not to have to worry about being poor in old age.

Sometimes I felt like Harry Enfield's teenage adolescent, Kevin: 'It's so unfair!' And equally frustrated.

Money was the pressing issue but that didn't mean I had completely lost the internal loop which kept replaying the sudden transition of husband, lover, friend to dismissive stranger. It takes a long time for that to fade. It fuelled hatred and I didn't want that. It got in the way of freedom.

Money. Money. I went to my desk and took out the papers the solicitor had given to me to apply for the legal costs loan. It terrified me, but I couldn't see what else I could do. I could end up losing my home, losing everything and still being in debt.

There was another court hearing, in London. I couldn't see that it achieved anything, other than more money spent. I didn't look at Nick so I don't know if he looked at me. I wanted to avoid seeing any pleasure in his expression and the not knowing what might lie behind this.

On the train home I tried to think about other things but when I stepped out onto the platform, it seemed as if my legs were reluctant to move. I forced myself to walk to the ticket barrier but it was as if I had completely run out of breath. I pushed on, found a taxi and got home, where I realised I was in trouble.

Chapter Fifty-Two

It was the middle of the night. A woman in the bed opposite me was enjoying an animated mobile phone conversation in a foreign language. I sat up in bed, the most energetic thing I had done for days, and shouted at her. Venom poured from me. I hated that woman, I really hated her. I had no idea who she was.

A nurse came quickly.

'She's keeping us all awake,' I said loudly, and slumped back on my pillows.

In the morning, the woman got up and paused at the end of my bed. She said she was sorry, but I scowled at her. What was wrong with me?

What was wrong with me? Over the next few days I had all sorts of tests. In between, Vicky and Sophie came to see me, and my man. I could see the concern in their faces, the shiny-eyed worry. But I really didn't feel as if there was anything amiss apart from complete lack of energy, and I had managed to summon something to have a go at that poor woman in the bed opposite.

Lying in bed, my thoughts were going through the washing cycle again when they alighted on something I'd heard, that women like me were prone to cancer after a huge shock and died within two years; I even knew someone to whom this happened. I stayed with this thought and realised that not so long ago I would not much have cared but now I did. I wanted to be there for my girls and for the new man, and, well, all that life was now offering.

When all the test results came back and nothing was there, I was allowed home. That was another thing, it felt like home, I no longer thought of the old house in that way, it was over.

Slowly, my energy began to return. New man wanted me to go on holiday with him, to visit his friends in Wales. I was still getting tired very easily but I was keen to go.

The next court hearing was not for some months so I decided to try and forget about it until I had to think about it again. The papers for the legal fees loan remained unsent and as my solicitor had not prompted me on this again, it somehow seemed less urgent. But I couldn't entirely dismiss it. There's that corner of your mind where such things take up space and won't vacate.

I liked the friends in Wales, and new man having them made me like him even more. We spent much of the time sitting round their kitchen table talking about the world and finding out about one another in this roundabout way.

New man and I also had time to ourselves and early one evening when we were sitting outside smoking and watching the day disappear, my phone bleeped.

I read the message and then passed it to him to read. We looked at each other and then we embraced.

Chapter Fifty-Three

Nick

Did I feel good about paying off C? It was a lot of money but if I'd had to keep the fight going, there was a danger the business would fail. It needed my full attention and I had not been giving it this for some time. The cracks were beginning to show, complaints which should have been unnecessary, staff leaving, profit and loss account starting to look sick. I knew I could turn things round but it had to happen quickly.

I say it was a lot of money but chicken feed compared with potential for the business. C's timing had been good as far as the business was concerned as I estimated it could be worth a great deal more within quite a short time.

There was Sophie too. I really didn't care about people like Jane, or even Vicky, but I was not prepared to lose my daughter. She never contacted me now and I realised there was little chance she would come and see me at home again, not since Simone had moved in and refused to meet her. I thought if I told her I had settled the financial side of the divorce, that I had paid her mother, we could be friends again. It might take a while but I was sure it would happen.

Things had taken their toll on me. I didn't have the stamina I used to but I suppose this was simply about getting older. Sometimes I imagined what my life would be like if I had not told C about the affair.

She was in part to blame, as I've always said. I'm not just talking about letting herself go, that had happened before and she'd taken action, lost weight. No, what I mean is her stupidity in challenging me over it, she should have chosen to ignore it, thousands of women, millions probably, make that choice all the time and everything stays in place.

She had taken a huge risk for a woman of her age. I had offered to let her go on living with me, I thought we could be friends, but she was so irrational. I think it would have suited her very well to go to bed each night with her book rather than with me. She could have Sophie's old room, or the spare bedroom, because Sophie would have kept hers if we had stayed together. The main trouble was I couldn't stand it if she touched me. I'd done that involuntary flinch when she had put her arms round me from behind that time in the kitchen, the week between when she should have known I was having an affair and when I had to tell her. I not only found her unattractive but repulsive, that was it.

I didn't hate her, not then, but it went that way as the divorce dragged on. She was such a fool. She knew me better than anyone and that I would keep on fighting her for as long as it took, and that I would win. I had warned her in an email, one of the last because she had stopped replying. It concerned me that she might lose her house to lawyers' fees, we both knew of cases where this had happened, but she was heedless, so be it on her own head. I no longer cared and had no intention of bailing her out.

No, it was the business which made me decide to settle. The business would always come first. I tried to imagine what I would do all day without it, and the prospect was bleak. I had no 'hinterland' as they called it, no hobbies, what was the point? Retirement had never been on my agenda.

Fortunately, Simone made few demands on my time. I had no idea what she did all day, only that she seemed to spend most of it upstairs. Perhaps she did this so as not to disturb me. I think she was grateful to me for having rescued her from her previous life. There was still the matter of her daughter, but I felt certain this would be resolved over time, as would things with her mother and sister. I wanted her to be happy but she had to find this within herself and accept, just as I had, that you couldn't have everything exactly as you wanted it to be.

There were times in the evenings when I caught an expression on her face that was sad. In the beginning I did my best to cheer her up but after a while I found this face of hers irritated me. I had given up so much for her, so why didn't she appreciate it more? She was free to do as she liked, go out shopping, spend more than she had ever known.

We didn't make love as often as before, but that was normal for a couple living together. And I must admit that my tiredness had a lot to do with it, getting the business back into shape was hard work. Added to this, I was having difficulty sleeping. I'd be thinking about the business and the problems would loom larger than they deserved, keeping me awake.

Tired as I was, one night I turned to Simone, reached for her hand and began what I hoped would make me forget about the problems. I think she must have been asleep because she did not respond at first and by the time she did, I had gone off the boil. I tried to carry on but it was no good. I turned from her and now found I had another worry.

I still couldn't sleep and in this state of exhaustion, coupled with wakefulness, every sound of the night seemed amplified: the night mail aeroplane going over the house, the distant clack of a train, Simone reaching for a chocolate.

'Don't.'

THE END

THE END